Richard Godfrey is a scientist who began working with elite GB sportspeople in 1991 and has been an academic at a university in SE England for the last two decades. He was born in Glasgow and brought up in Bearsden, a town in the West of Scotland. He discovered writing poetry 'by accident' in the 1970s and tried to apply a few of the lessons he had learnt during secondary school English classes.

In this way, creative writing served many purposes, including self-discovery, finding meaning in life, gaining a better understanding of the weather, natural history, work, relationships, disappointment, loss, and more.

I dedicate this book to the memory of my mum, Rosemary Forbes Smith Godfrey, who died in September 1980; to my dad, Daniel Heera Godfrey, who died in August 2024; and to my stepmother, Rosemary Neilson, who died in October 2024.

Richard Godfrey

SO LET IT BE WITH CAESAR

More Poems Providing Insights
On Life And What It Means

AUSTIN MACAULEY PUBLISHERS®

LONDON * CAMBRIDGE * NEW YORK * SHARJAH

A CIP catalogue record for this title is available from the British Library.

ISBN 9781037115240 (Paperback)
ISBN 9781037115257 (Hardback)
ISBN 9781037115264 (ePub e-book)

www.austinmacauley.com

First Published 2025
Austin Macauley Publishers Ltd®
1 Canada Square
Canary Wharf
London
E14 5AA

I would like to thank Linda Alexander, the person who strongly encouraged me to first publish and who continues to support and encourage me. We have known each other since secondary school, and I continue to enjoy and value our friendship, which I am sure will endure for many more years to come.

Thanks, too, to Carly Baird for reading my previous book and other poems, some of which are included here in this second book and, of course, for her consistent and very generous words on my poems.

Table of Contents

Preface

This is my second collection of selected poems, and includes a number writtenbetween the years 2016 and 2024. There is one exception to this: 'Grimaldi's Proud Boast*',* a narrative poem which I wrote in 2004. It is a moral tale about the 'dangers' of politics, relationships, emotions, and avarice of the human condition.

In general, most of the poems here relate to themes such as: understanding the world and your place in it, finding meaning in life, enjoyment of natural history, weather, health and exercise. One, *Echoes of a Life Left Behind*, resulted from the great sadness I felt in clearing my dad's house before sale and after he had been moved into a nursing home with Alzheimer's disease.

The majority, however, are concerned with relationships, politics and particularly those associated with work; the fact that I do not feel valued, and more than a little betrayed, in the workplace and my feelings about that. There are also poems in memory of my dad, who died in August 2024 after four years in a nursing home, and of Rosemary, my stepmother, who died in October 2024.

A colleague and friend, an academic from the university where I work, read my first collection and also the poem I wrote in memory of my dad, *Sparkling Memories*, which is in this current collection. Following some of my poems, especially the one in memory of my dad, he asked me to write a poem which reflected the relationship he had with his mother—as the elder son in a family of six siblings and without a father—who died when my colleague was 12 years old.

He is from West Africa, so it was a real challenge as we come from different worlds and different cultures, amongst many differences. But I gave it a go. It seemed to work out well as he liked it and said many of his family, friends and relatives had read it and thought it was 'great'. In fact, a few said it was 'uncanny' how I had captured the 'essence' that my friend was hoping for. So, a further development in my journey to become a poet in 'six easy decades'!

When trying to think of a suitable and clever (?) title for this collection, for some reason, lines from Shakespeare's Julius Caesar sprang to mind:

> The evil that men do lives after them.
> The good is oft interred with their bones.
> So let it be with Caesar.
> (Act III, Scene 2)

The last two lines struck the greatest chord, so I selected the last line as the title of this poetry collection—as it seems any good I do is ignored or devalued (at least in the workplace), and, to carry the symbolism to its terminus. It seems I have cast myself as Caesar!

I'm not quite sure what to do with that realisation. I'm sure many would proffer unflattering suggestions. As I age, however, there are fewer and fewer 'significant others', people whose opinions I respect and attach any value to. The mistake was to be affected by so many 'insignificant' voices for so long.

Recently, I have become aware of another reason why I write poetry. I need discussion and debate, and, in the absence of enough of it, I find writing poetry helps me to think things through, order my thoughts and, hopefully, perhaps also increase the chances that I will hold more honest views and perhaps even, better identify truth. In addition, linked to the idea that I want to ensure that any spare time I have is largely spent doing things that seem worthwhile.

There is a final slew of reasons which I have more recently become aware of and there are two facets I would reveal; one interaction with a close friend and colleague who died a few years ago at an old age, and the other is the work, in modern literature, that is recognised as a 'classic' of that genre. The latter is *The Gulag Archipelago* by Alexander Solzhenitsyn.

From The Gulag, Solzhenitsyn's work continues to resonate with me and includes the suggestion that:

"The strength or weakness of a society depends more on its spiritual life than on its level of industrialisation. If a nation's spiritual energy has been exhausted, it will not be saved from collapse by the most perfect government structure or any industrial development. A tree with a rotten core cannot stand!"

(As quoted by Konstantin Kisin in his speech at the inaugural Alliance for Responsible Citizenship (ARC) Conference in London, UK, 2023).

As a scientist with an appreciation of the many accomplishments of our Victorian ancestors—for whom science and art were but two sides of the same coin—I find an echo, a chiming, with Solzhenitsyn's words in the words of the British-American novelist Raymond Chandler:

"There are two kinds of truth. The truth that lights the way and the truth that warms the heart. The first of these is science and the second is art."

This, the former reason, results from this quote spoken to me by my good friend and colleague, Professor Craig Sharp. Craig was my senior (and better) by almost thirty years and is sadly, no longer with us. But many of us knew him as a university academic, scientist, physiologist, pathologist, sportsman and poetry critic, a trailblazer in many fields, short-listed for a Nobel Prize, and a polymath.

A man of unique and singular breadth and depth of knowledge that I will never again encounter, and it was a privilege to have sat, as a student, at his feet in awe and learnt so much over many years. Many consider me to have great breadth and depth of knowledge, at least in science. He was always humble, generous and just, an incredibly nice person. I am humbled to know that my knowledge is a drop whilst his was an ocean.

Craig pointed out these two sides of the human psyche: the rational, scientific, analytic, objective part and the creative, impulsive, spiritual, subjective part. I have been trained and spent all of my professional life immersed in the former, but I realise that there is spirituality in many of us, and five decades ago I seem to have stumbled over it in myself.

That the spiritual is a part, to a greater or lesser extent, of all humans includes those who lack overt accordance with religiosity, and often in them, this is realised and or expressed in art and more widely in the creative process.

I have been aware for decades that I have a deep-seated desire to seek truth and meaning in my life by exploring both aspects. I seek 'the truth that lights the way' as a professional scientist and 'the truth that warms the heart' by writing poetry, and occasionally prose, to express myself, to make sense of my existence and to widen my understanding. In turn, this makes me feel good, useful and purposeful. Both 'truths' together help provide meaning, and both together, I think, connect me to/with the spiritual.

Is this religion by another name? I identify as an atheist, but I have a lot of reading and writing to do before I can be certain of where my own beliefs and values really fit. As a man in my 60s who has not even begun to decode the signs and symbols strewn throughout the experiences of my life, and who has not found the answer for five decades.

As a man who, in fact, is only now perhaps, starting to ask a few paltry and ignorant questions in the right direction, I sometimes wonder if I will survive long enough to find that truth? I guess it amounts to the eternal question:

"What is the meaning of life?"

I doubt anyone has ever found an adequate, satisfying answer. So let it be with Caesar.

A note on the structure of this collection and on elements of style within it.

My first collection, *Secrets, Lies and Little Joys,* demonstrated to me how the presentation could be improved. Each commentary came after each poem, but this was not always immediately obvious. This was understandable as poems, and indeed commentaries, were not all of equal length, and this meant there were many times when a commentary was on a page opposite a poem that it did not relate to.

Accordingly, for this collection, *So Let it Be with Caesar,* I have placed a heading '*Commentary on—*' and stated the poem that the text relates to, and I have also attempted to have the commentary close to, or at least in close proximity to, the poem to which it pertains.

Incidentally, the point of the commentaries is multifarious: to provide insight into how or why I wrote the poem and, in some cases, some science, workplace or other 'niche' terminology that might not be familiar to the majority, who don't have a science background or who may not work in higher education. So, the commentaries also provide some explanation and clarification.

The reader can, of course, choose to read in any order: poem then commentary or vice versa. There is also the alternative not to read a commentary and instead, to let the poem stand alone and for the reader to extract whatever they wish from it without anything external that may alter the thoughts or feelings that reading the poem in isolation may generate.

There is an additional point. I think some people took all of my poems as serious when, in fact, some of them, or parts of some of them, could be described as light verse. That is, at times I am expressing things in a 'tongue in cheek' way, in other words, I am not always serious, aggressive or truly 'bile-spitting', although I admit, at times I do intend sarcasm.

If I suggest I might be violent to people, or forthright in my depiction of others or, if and when I appear to 'spit bile', it may just be for effect, i.e. a case of 'my bark being worse than my bite', or of exaggeration for effect. At times, you should imagine I say things with a wink and a twinkle in my eye. Perhaps we all take ourselves and life a little too seriously.

That said, I am sure there are ideas, opinions, and views expressed that chime with your own experience, so, of course, each individual is free to interpret and to view any and all as they see fit.

The Meaning of Life

I need not profound sadness.
I want not perpetual rain,
All I need for a happy life,
Is blue skies, warm days and a melodic refrain.

A lyric to accompany my heartbeat,
Music for my soul,
Purpose, rhyme and reason,
Let life not take its toll.

Melody beats a path right to my heart,
A refrain to mark glorious days about to start,
When winter cold is banished and spring becomes summer heat,
All time being marked by the rhythm in my feet.

For rhythm, rhyme and reason,
Powers all human life,
But all subsides and bows to love,
No more daily passing strife.

Commentary on the Meaning of Life

There is a lot to be grateful for and a lot to enjoy and be happy about. The best place to find all of that is in the here and now. Don't spend too much time 'beating yourself up' for past mistakes or worrying too much about what the future might hold. I doubt any of us ever truly discovers the meaning of life, but in each day, perhaps we can find meaning and take satisfaction and even enjoy that.

Perhaps it gets easier as we age, and we are more likely to avoid allowing the unattainable to dominate our thinking. Control the controllable and try not to get too exercised by those things you can't control.

Bourne End Barbers

I've been putting it off for weeks.
The need for a haircut, from my mirror now speaks!
So, off to the barbers in Bourne End.
Hair irritating ears and, increasingly, my eyes offend.
First in the queue, in fog and mist and cold.
Soon, sitting in warmth, the barber with a flourish bold,
Bows and gestures to the chair.
I sit and, in the mirror, meet my own stare.
With another flourish, scissors and comb begin,
To trim and cut, as on my chest, I rest my chin.
With clippers and hot towels and sprays brought to the fray,
A smarter new look is soon on its way.
Tomorrow will be another bright, cold winter's day,
And perhaps better humour will my hand stay.

Commentary on Bourne End Barbers

Light verse on a cold, frosty, misty February morning, after putting it off for weeks, I finally went for a haircut. For decades, I have visited any old local barbershop and paid the lowest price possible, and so, generally, you get what you pay for. Since the end of the Pandemic, I have visited a Turkish barber in Bourne End.

So now, I tend to pay a bit more and, as a result, it is always a pleasure as you feel spoilt and, in the end, they have cut your hair well…at least, what remains in my case. As a 'grumpy old man'. I often feel like I'd like to murder someone (smiling winking face emoji), and so the last line reflects that!

Three-Day Week

It was on a Monday,
That I faced a great foe,
Death wrestled me to the floor.
'Be gone!' said I and pushed him out the door.

The bravado is fake, I fear.
But the brush with death was real.
If I'd believed in God that day,
I'd have pleaded a pathetic appeal.

But life goes on, and I did too,
With many things now revealed,
Not least, the value of friends who are true,
Renewed vigour and purposes to pursue.

A new day, still-alive-Tuesday,
Sunlight vaporised the dew,
Blue sky; gently calming, comforting,
No clouds to spoil the infinite view.

In the aftermath, life seemed more precious,
And so then, I resolved to make time count,
No pleasure too small to be ignored,
So many joyous experiences to recount.

And so it was, to Wednesday I awoke,
Embraced by a calmer aspect, to a greater rosy hue.
There and then, I realised, in sailing the rough seas of life,
As captain, no approval is needed from the crew.

Commentary on Three-Day Week

I wrote this about the week I had a heart attack back in 2007, when reflecting on it in 2022, and what it has meant to me subsequently. In this, I thought about and realised what good friends really are; why I should value and enjoy life; and that I needed to be much better at living in the moment. Why?

Because that is where contentment and happiness exist, not having angst over previous mistakes or worrying about what the future might hold. In this poem, I also recognised that there is a balance to be struck, and to a degree, that is perhaps a battle between 'good' and 'evil'. But that is a matter of conscience, philosophy, and perhaps, too, psychology, and so has the potential to differ in the thinking of one person compared with another.

When I was growing up, my parents were quite strict, and the 'children should be seen, not heard' mantra was never far from our minds. To be fair, my parents never uttered those words, but my mother was keen that her children would not be a 'bother' to other people. As a result, other parents often complimented our parents when we were on family outings.

I think one consequence of this is that it was decades before I was able to take initiative in many aspects of my life without first seeking 'permission'. Perhaps it is unfair to blame my parents, and I'm sure it could just as easily have been the way I internalised it! Whatever the underlying reason, in this poem, I acknowledged that I no longer need to defer to others who have unsubstantiated opinions and who are often less substantial, in character, even than I am.

Hence, finally, I feel I have control of my own life with little reference to or need for anyone else's affirmation, and so I acknowledge that I am now the 'captain' of my own life— my own soul!

Flight

Insecta chatter, insecta call,
Insecta living life, having a ball.
A dart, a dip, a gossamer flurry,
A *Calopteryx* bluer than halcyon hurry,
A shiny fuselage, bright sunshine glint,
Deep black pools for eyes. Of thought, no hint.

Wings that buzz, wings that whine,
A bee, a mosquito, both nature's design.
There, a marvellous marmalade hoverfly,
Hangs, curious in the air, before passing by.
Halteres swing in tune with Newton's third,
Midges, in symphony, rise and fall, food for a passing bird.

Ladybird, stag beetle, weevil, bombardier,
Clumsy flight, it's obvious to hear.
In rare moments with *elytra* open, wings unfurl,
Safety gone, from a twig they hurl.
A leap into the void, you almost feel the tension.
Flight; they hang above the ground in seeming suspension.

Vesper, wasp, yellow jacket, gep,
Scavengers, irritating outdoor diners in late summer.
They fly with vim and verve and pep.
But swat them at your peril,
You'll feel their wrath;
A painful sting, you'll jump, babble and froth.

Commentary on Flight

Light verse on insect flight, which is, most often, fast and furious and a wonder of nature.

The sounds that flying insects make are often a combination of the wing size, speed and surface area. So, small wings with very fast beat speeds, like mosquitoes, tend to whine, bees and wasps with quite fast beat and moderate surface area tend to buzz, and big beetles with large wings that beat slowly have a distinct, low hum.

But big beetles only rarely fly, so I have only heard a male stag beetle fly, once in the middle of summer and about seven feet off the ground at twilight. Accordingly, I am quite familiar with and easily recognise mosquito, wasp, bee and fly wing sounds. But I do a double take when I hear a stag beetle flying. Simply because it is so unfamiliar and seems so laboured!

I use *insecta* as, in the Linnean zoological classification system, insects are in the class of arthropods termed 'Insecta', defined as having an exoskeleton, six legs, compound eyes and so on. *Calopteryx* is a genus of damselfly, a fairly common insect in summer, often generally known as a Banded Demoiselle, with males being a bright metallic blue.

Flying insects are descended from a common ancestor with four separate wings. In the true flies (Diptera), the rear wings have evolved to become *halteres*, each being a stalk with a knob at the end, and both act as gyroscope-like organs that aid flight control. *Elytra* are the evolution of the front wings to become wing cases or covers as found in beetles (Coleoptera).

The first line of the third verse lists the names of a few beetles. The first line of the fourth verse has three common names for the common wasp (*Vespula vulgaris*), the fourth is the French language colloquial name for it: 'gep'.

27 Mar 2021

Echoes of a Life Left Behind

I sit alone in my dad's house,
Empty of people but still,
Full of Dad and Rosemary's possessions,
And, with rising melancholy, I fill.

Possessions that represent,
A life quickly abandoned, but,
Not by choice. Illness and old age,
Has changed everything, and deep is the cut.

I look around and see my sister's cold hand,
Not knowing, nor caring about the significance,
Of thoughtfully placed items for practical use,
Not knowing, nor caring about such magnificence.

Now, after two glasses of wine,
And, with no other distractions, thought is in spate.
I mull and I remember many good times,
But sadness seems to dominate as I contemplate.

I am reminded of the fleeting nature of life,
One moment full-bodied and rich,
The next emaciated with a spirit broken,
Life immutably changed, wiped out, drowned in a ditch.

But, depressing as this sounds,
It is a timely tolling of the bell.
A reminder to live life to the full,
To love it, embrace it and declare it with a yell.

For as tragic as this current tableau is,
It is as inevitable as sand running out in an hourglass,
So, seize the day, live life to the full,
Try not to let futility be your life in one quick pass.

Commentary on Echoes of a Life Left Behind

In 2014, my father was diagnosed with Alzheimer's disease. His diminishing memory had been a growing problem, noticed by all, family and close friends, and, as was often the norm, his diagnosis came quite a long time after perhaps it should have.

For twenty-six years, he had lived with his partner, and I felt pleased he had been able to find someone else after my mum died from cancer in 1980. I began living and working in the south-east of England in 1991, and I still live and work there now. So, during that time, perhaps three times per year, I would travel to Glasgow and spend a few days with my dad and his partner.

With his partner, Rosemary, living there, Dad had a conservatory built on the side of the house, and it fast became the centre of socialising, being used most days of spring, summer and autumn. Dad was a very keen jazz fan. Whether from vinyl, tape cassette, eight-track or CD, when I was growing up, there was always music playing in the house, and Dad also played piano by ear and was really rather good.

When we listened to music in the conservatory of his house, Dad would often put on a CD and ask me in the first few notes who the singer or instrument player was, and when occasionally I got it right, it was to his smile and obvious pleasure and sometimes to his surprise, so he'd add, "Well done!"

However, it transpired he did this with a lot of his friends too, as revealed to me by them at his funeral.

I enjoyed those times of chat, music, good food and wine, and Dad and Rosemary's company, immensely and even more so in retrospect. At the time, decade after decade, how could you ever imagine it would all someday end?

When I wrote this poem at the time of clearing his house and, not too long after he'd gone into full-time nursing home care, Dad was 89 years old and barely seemed interested in music anymore; at least not to the level of daily excitement he once enjoyed.

That too was very sad, and doubly so, because it was so much a part of the fabric of the man I had grown up with and knew well. Whenever I hear jazz, I think of my dad and remember all those times, and the music that encapsulated so much of who and what he was.

11 Aug 2023

Two Wasps

Two wasps upon a window bright,
March up and down in vain,
Looking for an exit,
And frustrated, buzz a quiet refrain.

Escape is just inches away,
The bifold door is open wide,
But still they march without success,
And will do so 'til the ebbing of the tide.

Commentary on Two Wasps

Wasps are interesting, but maligned insects.

A friend once asked me, "What are they for, since they do no good?"

This is far from true, they are not 'no good'. In August, if we are eating outside, particularly sugary things, this will attract wasps. They almost exclusively eat sugary items as adults.

They do, however, remove many dead insect remains to feed to their larvae, which need the protein. But adult wasps are attracted to sweet nectar, and that is what they detect in your sweet foods. And this means that they are attracted to flowers, so they are extremely important pollinators too.

11 Aug 2023

Upper-Crust Riverside Town

The noise it builds;
In tavern-once, now gastropub.
An atmosphere that's good but loud,
And generally hard to find, but that's the rub.

In Henley dwell the middle class.
With upper-class aspirations.
Long gone the enthusiastic graft of youth,
And honest perspiration.

I do not wish to cast aspersions,
And admit my characterisation might be harsh,
But on Friday lunchtimes, this pub is packed,
And every workplace must be sparse!

Commentary on Upper-Crust Riverside Town

A lot of riverside towns on the Thames are very similar, and in general, it is where the more affluent live and/or work.

Be Brave, Speak the Truth

For many, self-delusion,
Is the despot crowned,
No honest self-reflection sought,
Weak opinion and lack of evidence abound.

But this is only corrupt and wrong,
To see the truth derided.
To make decisions, honest and true,
On only objective evidence can be decided.

To stand against a throng alone,
To have your voice ring out,
Declare the truth for all who already know it,
But to be that one lone voice requires a heart that's stout.

Can I be that brave, lone, strident voice,
To challenge others with the truth?
Many will shrink and creep away,
Others will fight, and shouts will ring uncouth.

This is where I must make a stand,
Not leave my pleas unheeded.
For, in the current and the coming generation,
Restoration of resilience is greatly needed:

Too quick to throw the towel in,
To hide from challenge stark.
But no worthy prize was proudly won,
By quaking in the dark.

Commentary on Be Brave, Speak the Truth

We currently live in a world where people's feelings have become more important than the truth, more important than reality. It is peopled by a small minority who 'shout' very loudly, and so a number of institutions take notice, and even take-action against those, including employees who do not 'toe the line' by stating that black is white under threat of 'cancelling' or even being dismissed from their job for contesting or dissenting.

This is all wrapped in the guise of being tolerant, but ironically, it is those calling for this 'tolerance' who are, in fact, intolerant of anyone who doesn't agree with them; without providing any argument that clearly presents a rationale. Of course, there is no logical argument and, even if there were, most/all of these 'activists' are too inarticulate to make it. As arguments go, 'because' is an infantile response.

We, quite rightly, expect more from adults who should live as thinking individuals. Who may not be entirely comfortable explaining themselves but who agree it is perfectly reasonable to be expected to, on occasion, explain themselves, especially if they are seeking a change to well-established and generally accepted norms.

When we are expected to disregard hard-won scientific evidence, much of it gained over decades or even centuries, the madness must be challenged and corrected. But who should do this? It requires skilful oratory and articulate phrasing to ensure the majority understand what the 'right thing' looks like, and in standing against the madness, currently, they put themselves at risk.

Seascape

The cliff remains in sight and sound,
A thousand seabirds wheeling.
Skuas mob puffins black,
From rainbow beaks sand eels, they are forever stealing.

The seaweed in the shallows below,
The rising ozone smell.
In those forests, baby denizens of the deep,
Crabs, rays, skates and shark eggs dwell.

Mermaid purses there abound.
Vibrating to the rhythm of encroaching and receding swells,
Hollow sponges and soft corals sway,
Like urgent church tower bells.

Tide waits for no man,
In autumn storms and pull of the moon,
The thrashing waters surge, but,
With climate change, they increasingly dance to a different tune.

Commentary on Seascape

I have no idea where this came from. I was driving, and as I was parking in Waitrose carpark near junction 4 of the M40, I had an image of seabirds wheeling over a sea cliff, and the words of the first verse came immediately. So, before getting out of the car, I wrote the poem.

8 Nov 2023

Cruel Sea

The wheelhouse was warm and toasty.
The deck, a freezing, rolling tide,
In winter on the high seas,
Calm bright sunrises are seldom spied.

But into a cold, dark winter realm,
Fishermen still must go.
A trawler with a wide-mouthed net,
A silvery shoal, on echo, still too far away to show.

Commentary on Cruel Sea

A hard and dangerous life of the trawlermen and women on the seas, fishing even in winter. I wrote *Seascape* immediately before stepping out of the car at Waitrose and wrote *Cruel Sea*, after shopping and stepping back into the car, before driving off. No idea why the sea theme for both, nor the compulsion that had me write one immediately before stepping out of the car and the other after getting back in the car.

Carve a New Niche

There *are* nice people in the world,
Into which, at times, I feel I'm hurled.
Some colleagues think me from an alien race,
Fear, I have an agenda; ignore the sincerity in my face.
And so, at times, I feel my strength wither,
But still, the plant deprived of water retains life's tether.
And so too do I, cling to life,
And weather each day's trials and strife.
But destined for better things, I must rise above,
Yet fear, in seeking pastures new, I'll need a shove.
It is becoming easier to say 'no', to rebuff,
Better use of my time; my health, a body buff.
The fact is stark, with HE, I have had enough,
And must plan an exit before my life is snuff.

Commentary on Carve a New Niche

In the twenty years that I have been in higher education, a lot has changed. The students as people have changed, which is not surprising. Society, with addiction to electronic devices in general and to social media specifically, is increasingly revealing negative consequences.

The main problem in HE, in my experience and opinion, is the 'acquiescence of the system'. That is, authorities generally, big institutions and government, seem very often to give in; to fail to enforce rules and regulations; and fail to recognise objective evidence appropriately. I assume this is because the authorities almost always want to avoid confrontation.

University is supposed to be challenging for students, and as teachers and lecturers, our job is to teach the skills that allow them to cope in an increasingly complex world, which is, in turn, increasingly dominated by 'the fake' and is full of misinformation.

Again, we need to teach them skills, including cognitive (thinking) skills, to allow them to tell the difference between truth and lies, and to review objective evidence appropriately, and not just give them all the answers.

14 Jan 2024

Victims

Higher education is lost;
It has lost its way,
Coerced into virtue signalling our compassion,
It's become a way of life, a fashion.

I no longer want to be a part of the problem,
To which every day we all contribute,
We need to teach students to be survivors,
Not victims, lame Tik-Tokers, celebrity social climbers.

I think we need to instruct them on how to give.
So that society might grow,
To ask, "What can I do to serve?"
To develop the science and medicine that we all deserve.

Leave victimhood behind,
Make bold contributions,
As a side effect, you'll be respected,
One day on Earth, human life will again be detected.

Commentary on Victims

We live in an extremely 'woke' age. Where many things begin with the best of intentions, such as extolling and encouraging equality and fairness, many are hijacked by those with less pure intentions. 'Woke' has, in my view, become what I would term 'ultra-PC' and, as such, often ignores common sense. I think it is a blip that will not last, and frankly, the sooner the better.

I am not sure how we got here. The majority seem unable to take responsibility for themselves and their actions, declare themselves 'victims', or behave as such, and blame someone else. In short, a return to the Marxist ideals of the oppressed vs the oppressor, which also assumes you are being denied your 'rights'.

I am happy to support the rights of minorities, but if there is no cogent argument, or worse, you are called a bigot, and the accuser then manages to avoid any effort to justify their position, this is surely just wrong. Only a child, when asked 'why?' answers 'because'. From adults, that is infantile and should immediately be dismissed.

If a reasoned, cogent argument is well-made for change—and is accepted by the majority of reasonable, right-thinking people, i.e. people capable of applying critique to appropriate, objective evidence—then fine, perhaps change is required!

Footnote

The point I am making here is not simply for effect. Research has been conducted over many years by Social Psychologist Jonathan Haidt (Thomas Cooley Professor of Ethical Leadership at NYU Stem School of Business). He has determined that engagement with social media constitutes a real threat to mental health.

Teenage girls, for example, tend to engage most with TikTok, and there appears to be a direct inverse relationship between that and the fall in IQ in that group as a whole.

30 May 2016

Heart and Soul

I gently consider truth in what I see, hear and smell,
Spiritually, and in every fibre, every thew,
I try to live my life as a scientist through and through,
But qualified colleagues with the same approach are few.

In most, a reluctance to review evidence prevails.
A service to ignorance, intolerance; the very opposite of divine.
Still, there are veils.
But truth and light do occasionally shine.

Da Vinci, be my role model,
Darwin, be my guide,
To change the world with kindness,
Shun ill will, being careful my desires to hide,
And, fingers crossed, to see a turning of the tide.

Commentary on Heart and Soul

I work with people who, like me, have a PhD, the highest academic qualification. One of the main aspects of that training and a part of the award of the qualification is a highly developed skill in evaluating evidence. So, it is frustrating that it seems like many are only using this hard-won skill in the narrowest of their professional practice.

Colour in Winter

Let no one tell you,
Winter is drab and colourless.
Although often muted,
Strident colours still surprise.
And, as days lengthen, it is clear to see,
Days of sunshine, growth and colour are on the rise.

Bright green and bright red canes,
Of growth in hedge rows,
The green plumage and scarlet cap,
Of the green woodpecker, in meadows it probes,
Whilst in the trees, its greater spotted cousin,
Hops up, bark and drums, its head moves in strobes.

On the river bank: tufted duck, great crested grebe, coots,
On the bank, graylag feed on emergent new shoots,
The metallic blue flash of a passing kingfisher,
Mistaken briefly for a spark or migraine aura; what a picture,
But real; it flits down the highway of a quiet, slow stream,
Hard to focus on, easy to doubt, abstract; as if in a dream.

Commentary on Colour in Winter

Every season has highlights for me. It is too easy to think of winter as drab and colourless. There is colour everywhere, even in winter. I am writing this commentary many months after I wrote the poem, but we are once more in winter. Just the other day (we are currently coming to the end of January), I was examining a concrete post encrusted with lichen of bright green, yellow and orange hues. We all just need to learn how to look at and appreciate nature.

Doubt and Fear

No achievement, big or small,
Meets with approval or cheer,
Only what I might have done better,
It's frustrating and difficult to hear.

One can only think, jealousy abounds.
But there is only one answer to such doubt;
Meet them with further success,
Then enjoy their shade of green and jealous pout.

Commentary on Doubt and Fear

There will always be people who will decry your achievements or refuse to recognise them or suggest they are not achievements at all since they are too simplistic to be recognised as 'achievements'. When it happens, we must learn to rise above such things.

3 Feb 2022

Stark Winter

Low, slow-rising cold,
Winter sun derided still,
By the rude north wind.

Commentary on Stark Winter

Haiku is an interesting and challenging art form: seventeen syllables in three lines, five syllables in the first and last line and seven in the second line. I am not sure I ever do it justice, but I'll keep practising. Despite the fact that it is not traditional, I always feel the need to give mine a title.

13 Feb 2022

Why Did You Write Them?

I shared some poems,
From a period stretching,
Back 45 years,
Some of pleasure, some of tears.

In a recent, thoughtful conversation,
I was asked, "What makes you write them?"
With little time to think, I reacted,
And replied with words I'd not wish redacted.

"If I knew the answer to that question,
I'd know the mind of man,
I'd own the keys to my own soul,
And forever reduce life's toll."

Commentary on Why Did You Write Them?

In short, writing poetry stopped me from self-harming at 15/16 years of age and provided a far better, more satisfying means of dealing with stress and anxiety, and is actually creative, which is a much better way to deal with your problems.

In writing poetry, I believe that I am a better thinker, better writer and have a healthier way to resolve, or at least lessen, my own issues. All this as a result of teenage angst over a girl in December 1977, which led to my first poem in February 1978. On reflection, it's interesting that I think I don't own the keys to my own soul…but then, does anyone?

24 Apr 2022

Chocolate Addiction

My chocolate addiction is fulsome.
Akin to that of the alcoholic,
And a lack of appropriate action,
Results in me feeling quite sick.

But still, I place warm chocolate,
In my mouth, and embrace the sweet umami,
To reject the sweet, smooth, satin coating,
Of palate and tongue would require an army.

Sweet, smooth, silky; texture grows,
When mixing with saliva,
Then, dam-busting, river-like, flows south;
A mistress I could never deny, so why try?

Commentary on Chocolate Addiction

Since I was a child, I have rarely denied myself chocolate.
If my parents bought it, it would be hidden or stored
somewhere and at times I would steal and devour it. I often
found myself in trouble as a child for this, and in recent years,
I have recognised the risks of sugar to my health, so I have
reduced my intake.

In the six months prior to writing this, I only occasionally indulged in the odd square of Lindt dark chocolate and felt so much better by embracing a low-carbohydrate ketogenic diet (LCKD) for seven weeks. And immediately after that, I even tried a 'carnivore diet', just meat, for a further thirty days.

In reality, I feel so much better without too much sugar. I am not sure 'extremes' would work for everyone, but that short introduction worked very well for me. So, less refined sugar and processed carbohydrates would be good for most of us.

24 Apr 2022

River, Springtime, Calm

By the languid river's sultry curve,
I stopped to admire the view.
Light scattered by a motor boat prow,
An open-water swimmer, cleaving the river in two.

And in that scene,
Rivercraft and folk,
With the backdrop of Cliveden,
A more gentle, worry-free life we invoke.

Glad to have chosen this route,
So much varied beauty to spy,
It is a rare day to be greeted with such luck;
Beauty capable of bringing a tear to every eye.

Commentary on River, Springtime, Calm

Perhaps it's my age, but I am increasingly finding more awe, wonder and pleasure in nature. I get a thrill from observing wildlife, especially insects, which I seem to be 'tuned in' to spotting. But landscapes, too, are a great pleasure as described in the poem above.

24 Apr 2022

Spring Woodland

In natural, breath-taking verdant green,
Cacophony assaults the senses.
Of sight and sound, and smell, you almost taste,
In calmness, not in tenseness.

The forest floor carpeted in bluebells.
A-nodding in the breeze,
Bearing rich hyacinth perfume to the nose,
A sweet, alluring tease.

Sounds are twittering and tweet,
Sweet syrinx's evocation,
To document nature at its best,
Seems to me, a noble occupation.

Commentary on Spring Woodland

Again, here I am appreciating nature in all its springtime beauty. Bluebells in early spring are an awesome sight, and if you are close enough to smell them, it is surprising how strong and how wonderful the aroma can be. I have always liked knowing that a bird's 'voice box' is called a *syrinx*. It is onomatopoeic and is easy to remember, for me at least, because even saying it out loud seems like you might imitate a birdsong.

New Era

It's not an easy *true dat*! thing,
To see an era end.
I no longer want to sing but for me,
Glib acceptance is not an embraceable trend.

A pause is what's required,
To help me find my way,
For now, an era ended,
Means a new one comes this way.

In truth, I struggle to come to terms,
With the Alzheimer's that's taken, my dad,
Sheltered housing for my stepmother:
Habits and comfort ended, not simply a fad!

With such change, it's hard to find new skin,
It might not sit too well,
It might be hard to live in,
Will all be well? It's far too early to tell.

Commentary on New Era

Change in life is one of those constant things. Sometimes things change very little over a long time, and then change might be rapid. Perhaps, decades with little or no change lull us into the false belief that things will be that way forever. When, however, the changes come, we realise nothing is forever and that is why we must live in the moment and enjoy every one of the good times.

16 May 2022

Poet 2022

Almost ten years ago, I recognised,
My poetry was barely a spark.
I was not then, nor now, sure why.
But since then, I have rescued that pastime from the dark.

I have, generally, not tried to force it,
But let thoughts and ideas, passion and feeling,
Guide my pen. And so, I hope,
I am more content as, with deeper thinking, has come
meaning.

Then, I thought the reason,
Was an acceptance of the past,
A willingness to leave it there.
But really, that is not true, I AM accepting of the past,

But decades of writing, sometimes in fire,
Have sculpted me, it's something of a fact.
So now, writing is a big part of who I am,
And so much more, I have become the act.

Commentary on Poet 2022

I enjoy my poetry writing, and I think I 'abandoned' it for a while because I saw it, for so many years, as a 'need'. So, it served as a 'crutch' to get me through dark and difficult times, to keep me sane. I also felt I could only write well when moved by deep emotion, and for a long time, my prevailing mood was, sadly, black and negative. When that need was gone, that is, I no longer felt full of despair, I felt happier.

Frankly, I had, in the main, begun to associate my poetry writing with despair and with a negative mood. I was generally happier in life and so, for some time, poetry writing 'drifted away'. When finally, I engaged once again with poetry writing, I found I could write about many things, not just when I was in a 'downbeat' frame of mind.

I still have occasional difficult times, but poetry writing can help me make sense of it, and makes everything easier or at least more manageable. But I found I can write about many varied things, so I used it in many ways: to heighten the good times, the richness of weather, landscape, animals, birds, insects, trees; nature in every hue.

Even music and the reading of literature are enhanced. In fact, everything is. The quality of my poetry writing may be good, bad or indifferent, but it makes no difference; it still helps me in difficult times, it can change my mood for good, and very often gives me pleasure.

The last two lines of *Poet 2022*:
So now, writing is a big part of who I am,
And so much more, I have become the act.

I am implying here that I am a writer, but I am reluctant to say so because surely a writer is one who undertakes *creative* writing, someone who has been published and who does it for a living? True, I have had many scientific papers published, I wrote them, but there is very much less creativity involved. There, the craft is to deliver instruction, interpretation and justifiable meaning, and to do so succinctly.

It is an entirely different process and can be dry and boring as free rein of the creative mind, using imagination to aid descriptions, such that the reader might know what the process feels like, is not relevant, nor valued.

If you read the work of scientists from 100 years ago (Nobel Laureate from 1922, A.V. Hill, for example), it does suggest that it was different in the past. Then, it seems that greater creativity was evident in the academic writing and publishing process.

Google defines a writer as:

"A person who uses written words in different writing styles, genres and techniques to communicate ideas to inspire feelings and emotions, or to entertain."

This definition does *not* today include scientists publishing a peer-reviewed paper. Outwith my professional work, my unpublished writing includes prose on natural history, my views on politics and other aspects of science, the arts and so on, and so I do use other 'styles and genres to communicate ideas, to inspire feelings and emotions, or to entertain.'

By that definition, perhaps I might be a writer, describing myself that way to others. However, it would seem something of a 'stretch' and just a little arrogant. But then, I had my first poetry collection *Secrets, Lies and Little Joys,* published in April 2024!

See the second-to-last poem in this current collection, *A Mother's Love, A Son's Awe.* It attests to a new development, and I am much more accepting that perhaps I am a writer/poet. A friend asked me to write a poem to reflect his relationship with his mother: a very new and very real writing challenge for me.

1 Jun 2022

Powerful Poetry

I dance around it.
That poem, that entity.
It is alive, it knows me,
My fear, my pain, my glory, my disgrace, my identity.

I think, or thought, I fear it.
But really, I don't know.
I rarely engage with it for fear,
It will lose its power to shelter me from winter snow.

And so, at times of need,
When courage threatens to leave,
I'll send it out, unleashed like the Kraken.
But quietly, I'll smile, happy, the whole world to deceive.

Commentary on Powerful Poetry

I wrote this about another poem I wrote called *Aka-i*. The term is Japanese, I have no idea what it means, but in a novel I once read, it was associated with a character who used the term to describe the skills of self-mastery he had developed with rigorous mental and physical training verging on mysticism. My poem *Aka-i* is something that I can read when I feel downtrodden, vulnerable, depressive and so on.

Reading it allows me to feel a tingle on the back of my neck and has skin prickling all over, and comes with a growing sense of confidence and self-worth. It somehow unleashes a power within me that is at times almost uncontrollable, or at least, that is how it makes me feel.

I view it with reverence and only read it when I need to be 'lifted-up'. I see it as potentially dangerous, because it has me on the edge of losing control and because, if I read it too often, it might diminish the poem's power.

Aka-i

Retreat deep into your inner self,
Find that core of strength,
That never dies,
That NEVER lets you down.

Be comforted by it,
Let it soothe and calm you,
Feel the tingle up your spine,
The prickle in your cheeks,

The hair standing on the back of your neck,
Blood coursing, sending strength,
Everywhere. Through your chest and back,
Along your arms, down your legs.

The spark was never extinguished.
The strength has always lived.
Deep inside and comes,
To protect and comfort you whenever you call.

Commentary on Aka-i

As a teenager, I started karate, and most of the friends I met through that sport were like me, for a while, obsessed with Eastern philosophy. So, I really enjoyed the Nicholas Linear books by Eric van Lustbader, *the Ninja* and *the Miko*. At one point, the hero, Nicholas Linear, some sort of spy, was captured by the Russians and was being tortured for information.

Being a trained ninja, and one who had explored and become trained in a number of the mystical arts, he learnt many dark ninja arts of 'Aka-i Ninjitsu'. One of those was that during torture, he was able to put himself into a deep coma and eliminate any susceptibility to torture and be useless to his captors in that capacity. The books made a big impact on me; having such mastery over oneself seemed something to strive for.

I did karate for twenty years, and although I thoroughly enjoyed it, I never attained those peaks of self-mastery owned by Nicholas Linear as described by Eric van Lustbader. The dream, however, never went away, and I wrote this poem about it. The poem itself does, however, change the way I feel! I genuinely feel I have an inner reservoir of spiritual strength I can draw upon. From starting to read the poem, I imagine the process described in it.

I can feel it energise and strengthen, and the feeling grows from the start to the end of the words. So, I *have* used it at those times when I have felt particularly vulnerable, and it always works. That is, it turns my mood from feeling weak and vulnerable to strong and invulnerable.

I read it only when I need to change my mood and internalise its power because I fear, if I use it too much, it will lose its power over me. All very strange and clearly something in my mind, but whatever the 'secret', I have learnt how to use it and using the words, I can feel changes in my mood and the feelings and sensations in my body.

Not sure if it's real, probably not, but I don't care, it works for me! So, perhaps I have learnt to harness some 'spiritual' power and turn it into a feeling of increased physical presence and power. Weird or what?

20 Jun 2022

Cryptobranchus Alleganiensis

Cold, silent, brownish-grey,
Breathing through folds of skin,
Many thought, to hell it was tuned-in;
Slimy, muscular amphibian.

And so alien to us,
It was deemed to have escaped hell,
And so, bent on returning, there was named,
'The Hellbender', to many children, that tale we'd tell.

Yet, not a denizen of hell,
But a dweller in a few US river basins,
A giant salamander, the biggest in that land,
Myth and legend, created to mask that which we do not
understand.

Commentary on Cryptobranchus Alleganiensis

   The 'hellbender' is a nickname given to the giant
salamander of North America (Latin name *Cryptobranchus*

alleganiensis), which, as an adult, can grow to be 30–74 cm in length (1–2.5 feet). Its nickname, the 'hellbender', was given at a time when people were afraid of things that looked fearsome and that they knew nothing about, and only rarely saw, so often myths became associated with them.

Why 'hellbender'? Because people believed it was 'bent' on returning to hell!

Hope Springs Eternal

In slow creeping cold,
And twilight's deepening dark,
A flame was lit,
From a simple, tiny spark.

It burned and burned,
A persistent, warm brightness,
To spite the sting of cold,
To banish biting wind carrying evil, old.

And soon emerged,
Hope renewed.
And in it, at first faltering,
Courage was in him imbued.

He spoke many an encouraging word.
In lilting song,
No more evil.
Pestilence, all gone.

Commentary on Hope Springs Eternal

Sometimes you have to recognise when things are good and, when focusing on good things, you might overcome an 'ill-wind'.

Old Haunts

I approach old haunts.
With a certain trepidation,
In case I meet those I'd rather avoid.
So, I visit with a certain reservation,
Hoping to avoid those of ill-intention,
Facing them and the aftermath of consternation.

To have to explain,
My history, my life,
Since last, I saw them.
To relate episodes of triumph and of strife,
Of how, at times, I rose above adversity,
But missed my window and a sane, happy wife.

In fact, I owe an explanation to no one,
No need to answer those of ill intent.
So many bonfires, left in the past,
With embers long-since spent.
No new identity needed,
No false stories to invent.

I answer to myself alone,
And enjoy a life of general content,
Where achievements are many,
Some are lost, I still lament.
But I've made peace with my own shortcomings,
And so, as minor failures, they elicit only minor discontent.

I'll not trouble you for answers,
In life, comes good and bad,
To spend time deriding your own conscience,
Is a path largely trodden by the 'mad'?
So, embrace a happy future, let the past lie dead,
Embrace all with smiles and joy; no reason to be sad.

Commentary on Old Haunts

Since my father went into a nursing home with Alzheimer's disease almost three years ago, I have phoned at least once a week to speak to the staff to hear how he is and occasionally to speak to him. However, since I live in Buckinghamshire and work in Middlesex, and he lives outside Glasgow, where I grew up, I now visit Scotland just once a year.

When in Scotland, I often wonder if I might bump into people I knew when I was living in Scotland more than thirty years ago. On this particular day, I had been walking on my own in Mugdock Country Park. After my walk and natural history spotting, I enjoyed a coffee in a café there and wrote this poem, hoping I wouldn't bump into anyone I knew in the 'old days'!

11 Aug 2023

Post a Weight-Training Session

My arms are sore,
My neck is worse,
I alter my position to get relief,
And to record the moment, resort to verse.

Whilst training is at times a chore,
It provides good health,
A challenge incarnate, never a bore.
More often post-training, I am imbued with a feel-good wealth.

I reflect and see inestimable value.
Each ache provides a thousand charms,
And each ache abates quite quickly,
It's why I choose to adhere to training strictly!

Commentary on Post a Weight-Training Session

Exercise is a must for humans. Dame Tanni Grey-Thomson put it well, interpreting real data by phrasing it differently: 80% of women and 70% of men are not fit enough to be healthy. And that rises to almost 90% in those 65 years and older.

The World Health Organisation (WHO, 2020) guidelines are for 150–300 minutes of moderate intensity; 75–150 minutes of vigorous intensity exercise or some combination of those per week; and everyone should be exercising at least thirty minutes every day. Increasingly, research evidence suggests that resistance (weight) training is the best exercise, although I suspect that in time, a mixture of aerobic and resistance exercise will probably prove best.

29 Oct 2023

The Spread of Falsehood

I do not easily,
Settle on the opinions that I hold.
I read and think and war with them,
Wrestle to find my own, not just accept whatever I am told.
But therein lies much conflict,
When contradiction is required,
Of arguments poor and weak and ill-informed,
Where false prophets are by management desired.

Commentary on the Spread of Falsehood

Thanks to the internet and social media, there is a huge amount of information available, and it is not all correct or truthful. We, therefore, need to become much better at distinguishing between unsubstantiated opinion and objective facts or evidence. And sometimes misinformation is used to divide us.

Betrayed by Most

I have no friends,
Left in that place.
When I am there,
I no longer recognise a friendly face.

I turn disbelieving,
To scrutinise the horde,
And see only green-eyed monsters.
Suspicion, fear, the false, hoping to be Lord.

But no open, honest,
Frankness, can there remain,
When forlorn, without hope,
They view their own existence with disdain.

But I am not part of that scene.
I still have hope,
And confidence in my own creative mind will still remain,
With unspoken putdowns, I can easily cope.

But to do so, I now,
Often absent myself,
The better to stay focused,
The better to succeed with stealth.

Commentary on Betrayed by Most

I'm afraid the workplace has reached that point where I no longer enjoy it and would often rather be somewhere else. Retirement is, however, something that will be a realistic proposition in the next three and a half years.

6 Nov 2023

Hips
Reflection 2023

The constant pain,
Was a drudge,
There were few analgesics I could take,
So, the constant pain I could not fudge.

Before bed, I'd take painkillers,
On paracetamol, I'd max out.
But too soon they'd wear off and I'd awaken,
And so, with weary, frustrating pain, I'd wrestle and I'd shout.

This did not ease the burden.
And for ten long years, I'd swear,
The world had completely forsaken me,
And in my heart was rent a tear.

Commentary on Hips: Reflection 2023

Most of my 40s were lost to the pain of osteoarthritis in both hips. I guess 25 years of karate, doing splits between chairs, etc., didn't help and brought on this familial problem early. So much so, surgeons were reluctant to operate because they felt I was too young and might, therefore, require more than one 'revision' in the future.

I could not take sufficient pain medication as I had a heart attack in 2007, and the medication I was taking for that was likely to be rendered less effective if I'd taken stronger pain meds for my hips. Perhaps that is an argument that should have been factored into the decision as to when to have a hip replacement.

I had ten years of pain, and for the last five years, the pain was sufficient to wake me every night, and it wasn't until 2013 and 2014 that I had my hips replaced.

Tarred With the Same Brush

You assume that we are like you,
And so, judge us by what *you* lack.
I am *not* like you,
I *have* integrity, and I know you will never have my back.

Tell me, have you always also lacked,
Honesty, honour, empathy and compassion?
It seems your DNA has not been tainted by these things.
To see them as frailties has always been your fashion.

Commentary on Tarred With the Same Brush

I can only assume that the reason we are dealing with a larger workload, year on year, is often as a result of very large increases in admin over the decades, and that admin seems simply to be, to confirm we are doing our jobs.

I am not sure why professional people would be required to do so unless they were not trusted, and where management will not confront individual wrongdoers. 'Do not assume we are like you' is addressed to management. In my opinion, *they* lack integrity and therefore assume that we, academics, are the same.

15 Nov 2023

George Gordon

From the train, I see the spire,
Atop Harrow Hill, where the school is,
Served by that same church,
And a graveyard where Byron lies.

George Gordon never knew the truth.
Of how enduring his name would be,
How long his poems would persist in the memory
A man among fellow romantics, no mere ephemery.

Commentary on George Gordon

George Gordon, Aka Lord Byron, is buried in the churchyard of Harrow School. Since I used to work in Harrow, I occasionally visited and found the small graveyard full of atmosphere; one that seemed to me to evoke the spirit of the great man.

16 Nov 2023

Haragei

I work to recover,
And develop the power of Aka-i,
To find it close to me,
But far from the sight, or ken, of others.

Most often, it ran parallel,
To my life. Only occasionally finding me.
Usually, in times of want or dire need,
When fire within grows to quench the fire without.

Now I fight to reclaim that time,
When, in my 40s, it felt like in water, and I was held under.
But now restored, and gaining back what was lost,
Ill-mood and frailty now to the four winds, cast asunder.

Commentary on Haragei

'Haragei' is like a sixth sense that has its origins in ancient Japanese spirituality. Many generations of martial artists have tried to capture it. 'Aka-i' is a legendary power that allows the owner complete control over their own body, even to the point of generating fire or putting themselves into a coma for protection.

26 Nov 2023

Evocative Winter Light

I awoke to winter frost,
To the east, an expressive sky;
The story of a cold, dark night,
That spoke to a breaking day of colour-not-shy.

The red and orange daybreak,
Bled into grey-white mist,
And the cloud above glowed with the light,
Of the sun, entrapped in a grey-clad fist.

Commentary on Evocative Winter Light

A beautiful sunrise on the road between Lane End and Marlow led to this poem. It was easy to see, or imagine, images formed as changing light and clouds became intertwined.

28 Nov 2023

Too Deep, Too Dark

If you read my poetry, you will know me,
Heart, mind and soul.
I am not sure that would be good for anyone,
And on all of us, it will take its toll.

In life, perhaps no one
Should know all you are;
The good, the bad, the warm, the cold.
To know it all, a bridge too far?

Commentary on Too Deep, Too Dark

In reality, a lot of my poetry, especially that which seems loaded with bile, is in fact light verse and/or is satire. At least, some of it is! In saying that, it is often also said that poets wear their hearts on their sleeves, or rather, they put it on the page.

17 Jan 2024

Mark Harries

Mark liked stories!
He particularly enjoyed writing short stories.
And occasionally, hearing a humorous tall tale.
I wonder what he would've thought of it all.

World and UK politics,
Would I feel exasperate!
But he'd briefly cogitate,
Before launching his opinion on fools, he could not tolerate.

Of my life, I'm sure he'd be forthright,
No ignoring of many a mistake;
Of Sam? He'd have metaphorically given me a shake,
Called me a 'bloody fool!' and asked if I was ever awake.

His legendary wit, acerbic.
He was a good friend too, despite the frequent expletive,
He took real pride when my PhD I'd completed,
Unfortunately, his prediction that I'd rise to prof is so far
defeated.

If my failure to climb that pole is a defeat,
I now think I might forgo promotion,
And wonder what he'd counsel, he'd create a commotion.
Perhaps he'd recommend more targeted devotion.

I continue to miss his company,
His wit and forthright wise counsel,
A whiskey and some quiet chat.
A real 'no-nonsense' man, not slow to say, "That's enough of that!"

Commentary on Mark Harries

With Professor Craig Sharp, Dr Mark Harries founded the British Olympic Medical Centre (BOMC) at the behest of Seb Coe, to set up a science and medicine centre to support elite GB sportsmen and women.

Mark was a chest physician and had been the Chief Medical Officer for UK Surf Life-Saving and a Medical Officer for the British Amateur Gymnastics Association. Mark became the chief physician in charge of Northwick Park Hospital in Harrow, where the BOMC was based.

He was a founding member of the British Association of Sport and Exercise Medicine and sat as chair of the Intercollegiate Board on Sports Medicine that, under his chairmanship, successfully set up a consultancy pathway for sports medicine in the UK.

He was a legend! He was the doctor who, on a flight at 29,000 feet, had saved another passenger who had a tension pneumothorax by puncturing his chest wall with a wire coathanger, and airlines used the medical manual that Mark wrote for decades.

I worked at the BOMC for twelve years and was chief physiologist for the last seven of those. Mark made it known how proud he was that I was the first person to obtain a PhD whilst working there.

Unfortunately, and ironically, Mark died from skin cancer, being a long-time surfer and often exposed to the sunshine. This seems to be somewhat ironic, too, as being a chest physician, he ran a lung cancer clinic every Tuesday! I was fortunate to be the one to have the obituary, which I wrote in his honour, published simultaneously in the journal of the British Association of Sport and Exercise Medicine and the journal of the British Association of Sport and Exercise Sciences.

8 Jan 2024

Alone

I was greatly loved,
But blind to that good fortune,
Now, I am alone.

Commentary on Alone

Haiku is the ultimate in succinct expression, and I am yet to do it justice, but I'll keep trying. This haiku expresses the realisation that many of us, when young men, don't know how lucky we are to have the love of a good woman. And, in that ignorance, we blow it!

What Persists After My MI

Perhaps surprisingly, the aftermath was overwhelmingly positive.
In the fallout afterglow, I thought about legacy,
Something expansive.
As the dust began to settle, the event was no longer substantive.

For months afterwards, I was relaxed.
I valued so many things, so much more.
I tended to ridicule, pretending it made me perplexed,
That such petty issues caused so many to be vexed.

But the mantra, "Most things no longer bother me!"
Was unfortunately, not a description that persisted.
Once more, I became preoccupied and remained exercised by petty things I see,
But at least engagement with a lasting legacy partially sets me free.

Commentary on What Persists After My MI

Again, I reveal my naivety. I would always have thought that a serious brush with death, one that is scary and extremely sobering, would change your views on life forever. Perhaps, even that was insufficient to permanently shift my entrenched, rheumy, jaundiced view of my world in the workplace. Better than, to use it as a foundation to 'step further away from the wood so I might better see the trees', to better put life and its meaning into perspective.

I look at friends with children; they have more responsibility than me; they are less self-absorbed, and they are more adult than I am! However, to avoid 'beating myself up' too much, they had no choice but to change, and I have had much less pressure, social and circumstance, to do likewise. In that, there are also lessons on the meaning of life, which, by virtue of being childless, perhaps I have missed out on!

12 Jan 2024

Ode to Greater Resilience

You think you create a storm in me,
And hope that it is a disorder that you see.
But only a breeze exists.
In fact, it is my self-belief that persists.
I no longer care what you think,
To spite you, from the well of joy I will drink.
I fear no stones you may throw,
With growing self-confidence, I myself bestow.
The stones bounce off without a scratch.
Green with envy, on me, you'll never be a patch.
And as the cold wind blows, its icy fingers I embrace,
I can enjoy the cold; in any case, it's something I can easily face.
Here is a place I no longer wish to remain,
Where increasingly, I'm greeted with disdain.

Commentary on Ode to Greater Resilience

My resilience comes and goes like a sine wave, and it has always been this way, but I do think the peaks are getting higher and the troughs are shallower than they once were. At one time, the suggestion that I am not sincere made me angry; now it just irritates me. But the 'imposter syndrome' at times persists, and sometimes I have to write my achievements down to 'shore up' confidence in my own ability.

But that seems to have decreased a lot in frequency. The good thing is that the group of significant others, those whose opinion I deem important, is diminishing. In other words, there is a smaller group of people whose opinions I respect or care enough about to listen to.

13 Jan 2024

Failure, My Friend

Failure was a friend to me.

In this, I excelled; everyone could see.

I failed my Highers, receiving just 'comp Os'.

For a lesser individual, there's a risk of mental decline, in droves.

And then, two degrees slipped from my grasp,

I gained the third after three years working, but, frankly, it was quite a task.

Three years as a lifeguard and swimming coach.

It was not my choice, but with other options, my life didn't hoach.

But many things were learnt and experience was gained,

To work shift-work and to coach, not things for which I wanted to be famed.

By good fortune and good luck,

At Glasgow Uni, I made my stand and a UG degree in my waistband, I did tuck.

Finally, back on track to be a Sports Scientist; my desire of old,

The next chapter of my story, waiting to be told.

Commentary on Failure, My Friend

My sister was always much more studious than me and was consistently a better student than me. She got five As in her Highers, but in contrast, I got six O-grades and failed my three Highers, getting just three 'complementary O-grades' instead.

That meant I had to go to Clydebank Technical College, where I took two Highers (biology and physics) and a laboratory technician's certificate, and, luckily, that got me into university to do a degree at Glasgow Tech in Applied Biology. After a year, I failed that and went to a college in England to do a sports studies degree and failed that after three years!

I then worked as a lifeguard and swimming coach for three years before, very luckily, getting back into HE. At the University of Glasgow, I got a good BSc honours degree (2.1) in physiology and sports science. During my finals, I was successful at an interview for a job at the British Olympic Medical Centre.

During my twelve years there, I was promoted three times and for the last seven years was the chief physiologist. Whilst working at the British Olympic Medical Centre, I successfully completed my PhD (The Exercise-Induced Growth Hormone Response in Humans and Its Association with Lactate) in 2003.

The difference between me and my sister is, I think, that I learnt how to cope with failure better, probably because I had more experience of it! However, whilst I wouldn't recommend that students seek failure in order to learn, as an academic, I feel we do not use it as much as it deserves. Using it would perhaps teach those who are poorly engaged to change tack and so be more successful.

5 Jan 2024

Poetry Spectrum

Poetry has function,
Poetry has form.
It can be placid, warm, fair weather,
Or cold, wild, unrelenting storm.

In function, it can warm the heart,
Elicit strong emotion, bring a tear to the eye.
It can make a dull day exciting and happy,
It can rock your world, rake up feelings, usher in bright, blue
sky.

In form, it can echo the singing of the soul,
It has rhythm, metre, rhyme,
A beat to accompany life's symphony,
To move your feet, to sustain the unrelenting march of time.

Commentary on Poetry Spectrum

Some people, in fact, perhaps quite a few of us lecturing
in HE, are on the autism spectrum. I sometimes think I am on
the 'poetry spectrum', but where on the autism spectrum, at
times, signs include social awkwardness—being on the poetry

spectrum is something I have made up to describe myself; writing large volumes of poor-quality poems which may occasionally be punctuated by good 'quality' ones!

I think of the quote, which I can't quite remember:

"If you give enough chimps sufficient time on computer keyboards, eventually they'll come up with the 'complete works of Shakespeare'!"

I have now written a lot of poems, and perhaps, the occasional good one emerges.

The Past
A Different Land

I thought then, ending our relationship.
Was the right thing to do.
And when, a few months later, you sought me out,
I rejected you outright and got into no stew.

I felt self-righteous for sticking to my principles,
For not resurrecting our bond.
It is arguably a decision made in haste,
But I have come to regret it, and of you, I was more than fond.

I recall so much, so fondly now,
Of those days, I did not then respect,
Did not recognise, or value, such love.
If I had that time again, perhaps I'd be less circumspect.

Commentary on The Past: A Different Land

Values, standards and principles are all very well. They
are important, and I am often shocked by the extremely poor

standards and values that others have, especially in the workplace and amongst students. In your social life, these are important too, but beware 'cutting off your nose to spite your face'!

In other words, sticking too strongly to principles can be bad when it means you criticise yourself to a greater extent, and hold yourself to much higher standards, above and beyond those you would apply to others.

Trying to apply standards which are, arguably, too high can also sabotage work and love life. In both cases, it is better to step back, view things with a little perspective, do not do yourself down, and perhaps be a little kinder to yourself and to others.

In the latter area (i.e. love life), it is easy to make decisions which you later, with 20:20 hindsight, regret and which at the time were taken 'virtuously' applying idealism. Perhaps experience and common sense should more often prevail.

13 Jan 2024

Leaving Failure Behind

Glasgow was a degree hard-won,
With serious graft and some occasional fun.
But much was learnt,
In physiology's immersive fire, deep knowledge was burned.
My mind forever altered, my thinking, brazen and clear.
I was able then to step forward with a rationale that was clear.
So began a twelve-year career,
Working with elite athletes, I did steer.
To this day, I have experience more than any.
In such work, my skills are now many.
Skills in working at home and overseas, in the field and in the lab,
Still, I am without rival and so refuse to be laid out on the slab.
Still, so much to offer to the world,
Not yet ready from the mountain top to be hurled.

Commentary on Leaving Failure Behind

I'm not sure I have ever actually completely 'left failure behind', but I certainly have learnt from experiencing quite a lot of failure over many years. Failure now does not 'destroy' me.

Although being turned down for promotion twice despite 32 years of professional experience, publishing world-leading research on cancer and on heart disease, remaining the most experienced physiologist in the UK, whoever worked with elite athletes, blah, blah, blah, and not being recognised has crushed me. I currently find it hard to think that I will completely recover. What does 'non-recovery' look like?

Well, it means I am looking to see what else I might do to earn money in my life, and actually, this close to retirement, I question if I really need to work to earn money! I may not actually need the money (?), but I do need purpose and mental stimulation. I have, however, also changed my views such that there are now far fewer people whose opinions matter to me or that I value.

10 Jan 2024

The Sting of Tears

My eyes pricked,
My nose burned,
I shed a salty tear.
But it will not be this year,
That I succumb to wanton fear.

But that will not stop emotion.
Bubbling from my core,
Like lava flows across the land,
In cold air, it hardens and,
To be like that, I make a stand.

Commentary on the Sting of Tears

Even currently, when watching TV and someone relates a 'sob story', I can shed a tear. Perhaps that is more likely if something sad is reported on the news or in a documentary. But succumbing in recent times to sad or emotional experiences of others is not a sign I am weak, soft or a pushover.

14 Jan 2024

Key Actions of My Mum and Dad

Suddenly, my parents had no confidence.
In the school that treated me with such indifference
And had given up on me,
But my mother had not, as all could see.
So, I was sent to a new school, in time,
Where, in truth, I failed to shine.
Despite that, it was their belief in me that counted,
And, little by little, eventually I refused to be discounted.
Failures continued for many years; I barely made the grade,
And oftentimes I felt my morale fade.
In 1980, she died; cancer took her life.
In grief and being slow to grow up, I continued to experience strife.
But the years passed, and finally, a degree, accolades, a PhD at last,
She'd have been stunned to see all that had passed.

Commentary on Key Actions of My Mum and Dad

Attending a school parents' evening when I was 13 years old, my parents were told that I wasn't very bright and would never achieve very much in life. My mother really wasn't happy with that assessment, and I was sent to an educational psychologist for assessment. The outcome was good, but Mum and Dad felt I should go to another school, which I did, but I didn't do great at the next school either!

The big takeaway, however, was that I realised and really appreciated my mother's unshakeable belief in me. I feel sure she would have been surprised that I finally got an undergraduate degree and 'blown away' by my PhD and career since then. That belief brings me pleasure, strength and motivation to continue honouring her memory in this way.

21 Feb 2024

Got to Get Out of This Place

Run, run for the hills!
Here, are too many hidden, growing ills;
Too many bad actors,
Too many despotic detractors,
Troubles too great to carry,
Ideas I can never wed, never marry.
In growing isolation, I seem to dwell,
Daily, this place looks more and more like hell.
It has been a long time since the need for change.
Before infection adds to mange,
Before the day comes to a close,
Before the side effects exceed the dose,
I've got to get out of this place,
Now, frankly, paltry, any concern for losing face!

Commentary on Got to Get Out of This Place

Increasingly, higher education is becoming a more difficult place to work. The days of trust, that is, the days in which academics were trusted to rely on their own integrity, are gone, and we have to keep detailed records for 'annual monitoring'. In effect, we are contributing to the information designed to make a case against us.

If a small number of people, or even a single individual, transgresses, the correct approach would surely be for management to challenge the transgressor(s) and make sure they don't transgress again. Instead, however, whole processes are changed or new ones enacted that affect many who have done nothing wrong. That is so that weak management does not actually have to confront the very few real wrongdoers.

21 Feb 2024

Retirement Equals Boredom?

A 'nutcase' stalks the halls.
In a woolly bobble hat,
Anxious look upon her face,
She is clearly waiting, staring, on the edge of a seat, just sat.

I noticed her anxious, shaky steps.
As here, in the café hall, she stalked,
Looking for a table amongst the hordes.
Up and down the tiled cream floor she walked.

Wednesday 'elevenses' in John Lewis'
I should have known there would be a horde,
I felt both discomfort and reassurance,
For retirees, a trip to John Lewis', no longer getting bored!

Commentary on Retirement Equals Boredom?

I went to a local John Lewis store and sat in the café observing, and it seemed clear that a number of retired people go there for elevenses! I thought of my own retirement and hope I am not one of them for want of something better to do with my time!

7 Mar 2024

Annual Haematology Check-Up

Today I walk London's,
Early morning streets;
Killing time, getting exercise
Ahead of walking NHS beats.

I see smoking and vaping seem.
To have dramatically increased;
Boris' *sensible British public*,
Sooner rather than later, to join the deceased.

It's a cold day but, thankfully, dry,
But still too warm for early March.
Blossom, already out for two weeks, makes me sigh.
Climate change, in little doubt,
No great prediction; dry spring, summer drought.

Commentary on Annual Haematology Check-Up

In March 2010, following the discovery of the cause of
the heart attack I'd had in 2009, I had an (almost) annual

check-up by a specialist at University College Hospital. On this particular day, I arrived early after a long walk from Marylebone (down Edgeware Road and along Oxford St and up Tottenham Court Road) and had a coffee in Pret á Manger, a stone's throw from the hospital. What I saw on my walk and through the window of Pret led to this poem.

10 Mar 2024

An Early Year

It is really too much.
Such a mild first three months to the year,
Is not normal, not right and is of real concern;
Many plants in leaf, insects out of hibernation, cherished and
dear.

But for tree, blossom and daffodils,
To flower in mid-February, a month too early,
Will be problematic if frost comes again.
Too soon, the start of spring's hurley-burley.

Leaning on a farmer's gate,
I enjoyed the murmuring, burbling and whistling,
Vocalisations of skylarks when standing here last summer,
Now only heard, but surely too early in the season to stridently
sing?

Commentary on An Early Year

This poem expresses surprise and a little concern about
climate change and the appearance of spring seeming to come
earlier and earlier each year. In saying that, with more

education, I can agree with the contention that the extent of the problem and its cataclysmic consequences are overblown. There are more important problems to be solved with the limited resources available.

The most important of these is the education of women in developing countries. This would lift everyone out of poverty and benefit humanity most as it would free up more people to think of solutions to problems which are tractable, if one still references Maslow's *Hierarchy of Needs*. In other words, someone worrying about feeding themselves will not see climate change as a priority.

14 Mar 2024

Job Sell-by Date

Perhaps no one should,
Remain in the same workplace,
For more than ten years. Longer and,
Familiarity breeds contempt; you more easily lose face.

Respect and value, lost,
Growing contempt, ridicule, blame.
Experience ignored, you're seen as a boorish bore,
Others, jealous, find excuses to defame.

I am a survivor; I have no desire,
To claim victimhood for myself,
But increasingly, the over-sensitive zealots,
Threaten to reject me, to leave me on the shelf.

Commentary on Job Sell-by Date

Every job has its frustrations, but as a lecturer in higher education, it feels like a commitment beyond simply earning cash. Many of us talk of 'not letting down students' but over many years, it feels like servitude and that overused phrase used by management to guilt-trip, to manipulate and 'milk us dry', whilst under-paying people with true expertise.

18 Mar 2024

Ever Constant Cycle?

As the sun rises daily,
Over mountains, over sea,
The moon drags the tide twice,
There's no questioning, it will always be.

The seasons, so stark,
In this, the country of my residency,
Winter, spring, summer, autumn, locked-in. Pre-programmed?
But recent changes question: will it always be?

The cycles of nature
Are etched on each and every tree.
Things now are measurably different from my childhood,
And now I know, it cannot possibly always be.

It is life, striving to persist.
Interacting with, dominated by, paying its subservient fee,
To respond to the primal, physics,
The origin science, dictating entropy. So, it cannot possibly
always be.

Commentary on Ever Constant Cycle

When you get a substantial way through your life, looking back gives the impression of many constant themes, and the weather is one of them. The weather seemed predictable and reliable when I was growing up. Describing the UK weather seasons' temperatures by the rhyme 'five, ten, twenty-one, winter, spring and summer sun' was fairly accurate, just like 'April showers' and snow in Christmas.

Due, at least in part, to the human contribution to climate change, we are now more likely to have flooding in December and January. More storms, and many of them more severe, throughout the year and summer high temperatures which are beginning to creep above 40° C even here in the UK, once renowned as the epitome of a maritime climate.

6 Aug 2024

Transients 2

The eagle's feather, the butterfly's wing,
The mayfly's flight, the cicadas that sing.
The spider's web, a hair on your head,
The buds of May, a night in bed.
Love's perfect dream.
My mother's life ended; with frustration I scream.
My life's ebb and flow, but on and on?
My life's like water that may soon all be gone.
Spring seems too fast for me to truly savour,
So soon gone, not enough time to enjoy its flavour.
The lesson is obvious, it's really clear,
Live in the moment to banish all fear.
Too easy to become detritus, clogging the drain,
Instead, quietly hum this moment's strident refrain.

Commentary on Transients 2

In August 2009, when I originally wrote a poem I called *Transients*, the 'driving force' was an urge to recognise the ephemeral nature of life. With a further fifteen years of life and experience and reading, I ask myself what was to be learnt from that difficult time in my life.

As well as expressing myself more clearly, I also felt that paying greater attention to metre, rhyme, and rhythm could add further impact. So, I chose to 're-verse' it in the form of a sonnet (fourteen lines and rhyming couplets). This greatly added to my enjoyment of the process, which was therefore both exhilarating and satisfying.

28 Jul 2024

Life Hangs in the Balance 2

How tenuous, the hold we have on life
And yet insist on stress, war and strife.
If only we knew, daily life hangs in the balance,
Our perspective, we'd change, we'd take a bold stance.
The company of good friends and a life absent from threat,
Our woes would evaporate, no more with worry beset.
We'd see the value, enjoy such freedom,
In life, just a single thread protects us from tedium.
Let the scales fall from your eyes.
Be no more burdened with heartfelt sighs.
"Life is short!"
"You're a long time dead!"
Sayings to ensure it's with food from the tree of life we are
fed.
Too blind to the good, too wounded by the bad,
But, to not bask in warmth, sunshine, and good company, is
simply mad!

Commentary on Life Hangs in the Balance 2

I wrote *Life Hangs in the Balance* many years ago. It didn't rhyme, and so I built upon it to form this new poem. I feel *Life Hangs in the Balance 2* is, by using six more lines, more balanced in content, and the sonnet form adds better to the sounds, meaning and tone, when read aloud.

30 Mar 2024

Darkness Magnifies the Light

Some enjoy the darkness,
For the contrast it brings,
Making the light so much more magnificent,
Step from shadow, and your soul sings.

In sunlight, warmth is so much more,
Pleasurable when stepping,
From frost-etched shade.
UV on skin and soon vitamin D is made.

Commentary on Darkness Magnifies the Light

I feel we need to enjoy all of the seasons. We are lucky in the UK to always have had distinct seasons, and even if the demarcation is blurring somewhat, we do still have seasons. However, if the long dark winter months are bad and evil is 'dark', we need these things to contrast the good and the light. In every life, some rain must fall, so that way, we really learn to appreciate the good times.

Solitude

With ageing, you learn,
As friends have families,
And you don't, the dynamic changes.
It is the natural order, not simply one of life's anomalies.

I make the observation, with no 'edge',
No resentment, certainly no malice.
Perhaps an occasional mild regret, a little envy,
But I share responsibility for not drinking from that chalice.

So, it is natural and appropriate.
For those friends to cherish family time,
And, natural that I spend much more time on my own,
And so, I must capture solitude's benefits and make them mine.

Commentary on Solitude

There are many times when I actually enjoy being on my own, not all the time, but most of the time. I am generally good at entertaining myself and could do so, assuming I have books to read and a notepad to write on, even without electricity or electronics. And, of course, there is walking in the great outdoors in nature, a love that never ceases to interest me, and continues to cause awe and wonder and which calms my restless spirit when it needs calming.

5 Apr 2024

Hope over Experience

Where hope triumphs over experience,
I will open my heart.
A warm and pleasant land beckons,
A happy life, no adversity that threatens.

Where hope triumphs over experience,
I will make a new start.
No need for an eye on the past,
No need for hypervigilance, my happy future is looking vast.

Where hope need not triumph is in the moment.
Hope is an expectation for the future.
True happiness is in the here and now.
And to make the most of every moment is my vow.

Commentary on Hope Over Experience

I'm afraid I think the pursuit of happiness is an empty and vacuous quest. It is far better to find constructive things to do, and things for which the *consequence* or *side effect* is to make you happy. Assume the best, and often the best arrives. That is, constantly try to live in hope. If you are spending too much time with people who choose not to live in hope, or are mostly negative, perhaps rethink who to spend your valuable time with.

Life is too short to often think the worst is about to happen. Resolve to look on the bright side as often as you can. My mother was the one who had a saying for every occasion.

It was not my dad's preserve, and yet I remember him telling me, "Laugh and the world laughs with you, cry and you cry alone!"

Healing or Destroying

Is the process of writing,
Healing or destroying?
Rupi Kaur suggests you cannot always tell.
But I think you can, but sometimes in a quiet voice, sometimes a yell.
The message is revealed; sometimes on swell, sometimes on flood.
Even writing on the entirely negative prevents being mired in mud.
Write it down, put it aside, do not imagine from things you must hide.
Detritus, still there, but increasingly diluted by the tide.
The ebb and flow of life demands sight,
Of all, good, evil, rich, poor, wrong, right, good times and shite.
At one time, I found it hard to be discerning.
But you cannot go through life for everything, yearning.
A step back, being grateful for the best of times,
Because even bad times help identify a better path, a life divine.

Commentary on Healing or Destroying

I find my attempts at creative writing generally result in good and positive outcomes, and can be therapeutic, even healing, at least for me. Even if the topic or theme is negative, putting it on the page and then putting the paper away frees my mind and reduces the risk of overthinking things.

Myths and Legends

Hippolyta, hear my plea,

My feelings are obvious to see.

I yearn, a hopeless, forlorn hope.

Desire, a growing sensation with which I'll never have to cope.

She, the goddess, the ideal fantasy,

Remains only in my mind, there to dwell in ecstasy.

Then, to awake, to greet the dawn,

To have tasted the elixir from the well of happiness, drawn.

Far behind the gates of hell,

From where you escaped with a mighty yell.

Affirm the might deep within,

No one is immune from sin.

But you can rise above the rest,

For they lack thought and are of heart and soul bereft.

Commentary on Myths and Legends

I occasionally regret not having found a life-partner, but the regret is rare and fleeting. I have had a number of good relationships, and as Tennyson wrote in *In Memorium A. H. H.*

I hold it true, whate'er befall;
I feel it when I sorrow most;
'Tis better to have loved and lost,
Than never to have loved at all.
(*In Memorium A. H. H.*, 27.13-17)

30 Apr 2024

Vampire Supper

Get out of my face,
You useless fake.
You're a vampire, you're a ghoul.
Is it the thought of goulash,
Or two dead mice that make you drool?

In daytime, you're a long-dead corpse,
At night, all bets are off.
You rise and in your blood lust,
Confuse metal for meat.
Keep that up, and soon you'll acquire a taste for rust.

But vampires are a fearsome breed.
And for centuries they appal.
But meet a gay one in the Southern States,
Before tasting your blood, they'll greet you with a "HI y'all!"

Commentary on Vampire Supper

Comic/nonsense verse. There is no explaining to be done, and I'm not sure which obscure part of my mind it came from, or why!

23 Nov 2024

Storm Bert

Dark, grey, brooding, cavernous sky,
If there's been a blink of sunshine, it's passed me by.
Despite a warm southerly breeze,
The gusts are strong and batter all the trees.
Even under the canopy, there is little shelter,
As leaves, twigs, and branches are blown helter-skelter.
It is all at once: exhilarating and terrifying,
Birds in fighting flight, trees stand but cannot be defying,
Now rain lashes river, road, country path; each and every byway,
Fewer pleasures here now, on weather-beaten highway.
Shelter calls, I turn for home, the wind now at my back,
In a worsening storm, the enemies begin to stack.
I am being called home.
And for the rest of the day, will judiciously cease to roam.

Commentary on Storm Bert

I knew the storm was on its way, even when I set off for my walk, but it was exciting, and I am glad I did it but I avoided the route through woodland, which I commonly take.

6 Aug 2024

Sparkling Memories

In happier times, again we'll meet.
Beyond this dark horizon, the stamping of our feet.
Beautiful, bright skies will reign,
From blame and accusations, we'll refrain.
Instead, in equatorial evenings, lapping water on the shore,
The bar on the sand, a warm tropical sea breeze to the fore.
Whilst quaffing white wine, mojito, Coke and rum,
To the rhythm of Latin music, to syncopated hum.
It matches the rhythm of our souls,
Whilst the rhythm and the music halt life's tolls.
And then, to Dad's conservatory I return,
For almost three decades, jazz always on 'slow burn',
So consistent, a persistent trend,
A hard lesson: all good things must come to an end!

Commentary on Sparkling Memories

My dad sadly passed away on 3 August, ten years after being diagnosed with Alzheimer's disease and after four years in a nursing home. Reflection on the decades of regularly visiting him and my stepmother in Scotland resulted in me writing this. However, its origins are found in some thoughts, memories and events that began more than a quarter of a century ago.

An ex-girlfriend and I had an evening meal in a tapas bar in Chalk Farm in 1996. Spanish language, Latin jazz played in the background. We loved it, and I knew my dad and Rosemary would love it too. I asked what it was, and we were told it was Gloria Estefan's Spanish-language album, *Mi Tierra*.

A few days later, I bought a copy for myself and one for Dad and Rosemary, and we often listened to it in Dad's conservatory.

I'd visit from England three or four times a year, and I thought times like that would never end. There, in listening to *Mi Tierra*, I often imagined we—Dad, Rosemary, and I—might one day sit at a beach bar on some tropical shore and enjoy a drink, feeling the tropical breeze and absorbing Latin jazz.

This poem is a tribute to my dad and to that fantasy, which I still enjoy in my mind. I can smell the jasmine, bougainvillaea and hibiscus on the warm sea breeze, and it is a pleasure to see Dad's restless foot tapping against the bar stool as he is lost intermittently in the rhythm and the music.

Rosemary

She was my dad's choice,
A good choice, and true.
For he loved her, and she shared his life,
For decades, for all to view.

She always had a kind, warm heart,
But a saddened demeanour sometimes showed,
As from childhood, she bore scars on her heart and mind,
And over many years, the tears had flowed.

Despite difficult and troubled times,
Of which most were unaware,
She smiled and laughed,
And gave the impression that she lived without a care.

But, despite the pain and the sadness,
For others, she had many a kind word so fine,
And I was one of the lucky, as many a time,
As a stepmother, on me her love did shine.

Commentary on Rosemary

My father was very lucky to have two very successful relationships, each lasting more than a quarter of a century. Both women were called Rosemary, and my dad sometimes referred jokingly to them as Rosemary 1 and Rosemary 2. The first Rosemary was my biological mother, who sadly passed away with ovarian cancer in 1980, and it is the second Rosemary who is the subject of this poem.

She was one of the few people whom I have been happy to give my poems to read, and she read many of them in the last thirty years. She seemed to like/enjoy them; she was always interested in discussing them and very often said positive and encouraging words about them.

Sperm Whale

The whale looked,
Upon the face of the deep,
And dived. Down, down, down,
Soon, only its own secrets will it keep.

The warm sun of the surface,
And the upper ocean layers,
Going. The water, getting colder, and down, down, down,
Nothing yet in focus, despite hard stares.

The twilight envelops all.
But still from the eye, surface light now a mere glint.
Down, down, down; the dive goes on,
In fading light, flank dark as hard grey flint.

Soon, the dark and cold are all around,
And silence rules the deep.
Soon, clicking, rapid echoes sound, down, down, down.
And now, in search of tentacled prey: further secrets to keep.

For search, as we might,
We cannot find,
Colossal and giant squid. We cannot go down, down, down,
Like sperm whales, large heads, melon-lined.

The perils and the monsters of the deep pepper human thought,
And, by hooks and suckers, their flanks are scarred,
Far below, down, down, down, in massive fights for food.
It is their normal life, for the greatest part of millennia, left unmarred.

Commentary on Sperm Whale

Here I try to imagine the life of the sperm whale (*Physeter megacephalus*). Most of its prey is found below 1000 m depth, and almost 80% of its diet seems to be Colossal (*Mesonychoteuthis hamiltoni*) and Giant (*Architeuthis dux*) squid. They live more than seventy years and have the biggest brains of all species on Earth.

Increasingly, scientists believe they have their own language and even culture, which is probably passed down through the generations spanning 100s of years. Most sperm whales bear scars on their bodies, and these seem to be from the hooks on the inside edges of suckers on the tentacles of the very large squid species, which it seems, they must fight and overcome to survive.

16 Oct 2024

The Question of Elder Wisdom

They've stopped listening,
My words no longer seem to resonate, nor stimulate,
Younger colleagues who know it all.

Blindly repeating endless past mistakes.
They think both novel and new together pulsate,
They've stopped listening.

Rarely knowing or acknowledging error.
Nor recognising the wisdom of a man in elder state;
Younger colleagues who know it all.

With a gesture and a flourish bold,
Not just think they're right but know and hate,
They've stopped listening.

So, mistakes accrue at a pace,
Contributing to civilisation's demise, not adding hate to satiate,
Younger colleagues who know it all.

And so, I say, "To you of arrogant aspect, almost immutable
Find a little humility, act on elder experience!" But too late,
They've stopped listening;
Younger colleagues who know it all.

Commentary on The Question of Elder Wisdom

My first attempt at a villanelle. In the workplace, despite more than thirty years of unique, hard-won experience, earned through hard work, including managing others working with elite athletes and two brushes with death. I feel sidelined.

I've broached this theme before and thought about it often enough that, for me, it is now a 'stale' line of thinking. So, looking for a novel way to express myself, I chose the extremely challenging villanelle form.

The Robert the Bruce Playbook

Don't be too quick to throw the towel in,
You have not yet lost, so stand on your feet;
If at first you don't succeed, try, try, try again.

You cannot claim a victim's spin,
You can fight and banish all defeat,
Don't be too quick to throw the towel in.

Face the foe, chase and catch the hen,
Seeking knowledge can be neat,
If at first you don't succeed, try, try, try again.

Be prepared to work hard, push the door and come in.
From achievement don't retreat,
Don't be too quick to throw the towel in.

Hard work will get the job done when teamed with other men,
Success just breeds success,
If a first you don't succeed, try, try, try again.

Don't fight for what you want in vain,
Fight with heart and soul,
Don't be too quick to throw the towel in,
If at first you don't succeed, try, try, try again.

Commentary on The Robert the Bruce Playbook

An attempt to persuade the next generation of the need to develop greater resilience. This is the lesson from the telling of Robert the Bruce, the Scottish king's defeat in battle before his final victory at the Battle of Bannockburn in 1314. Bruce was hiding in a cave after losing a battle and, watching a spider not giving up, took the lesson to heart and today, most of us as a result are aware of the maxim:

"If at first you don't succeed, try, try, try again."

26 Oct 2024

Warning
Sense of Humour Failure

It's thanks to a relative stranger,
I hope to halt the rot,
For death and gloom and doom,
Have recently dominated each and every thought.

Time to review, to stop and to take stock.
Fine to identify the problem, and fine too, to talk,
But now it's time to take action,
Now it's time to walk the walk.

Re-engage with humour,
Cast a little less jaundiced eye,
Take myself less seriously,
My recent demeanour to defy.

Commentary on Warning: Sense of Humour Failure

My dad died on 3 August and my stepmother on 19
October; both within virtually two and a half months. It's

caused me some real consternation and sadness, and that, coupled with being turned down for promotion three times in the last four years, simply keeps the black cloud over my head.

I always had a laugh with my dad and Rosemary, and they wouldn't now approve of my sense of humour failure and the fact that I am taking everything, including myself, far too seriously. It was an acquaintance, Rich, whom I'd got to know as a regular in the same coffee shop I often visit. He suggested I might have lost my sense of humour.

To be honest, in recent times that has been true and I hope it is a 'blip', or rather, I need to be proactive and ensure it is only a blip!

Belief

It seems late in the day.
To question the belief,
I've been committed to for decades,
And so, atheism remains chief.

But the death of those who were close,
And my own near-death experiences,
Make more in-depth reflection: stark.
So, it is a new line of enquiry on which I embark.

Dawkins has been a long-time prophet.
With whom I've often agreed,
But increasingly, I found his voice too strident,
Some truths he spoke well, but in many he decreed.

In general, organised religion I despise,
Too easily corrupted, home of the corrupt;
Most Abrahamic religions are unwilling to compromise,
I'd shed no tears at organised religion's demise.

Too much tradition, enshrined in ritual.
Too tribal, too cocksure, too judgemental.
All in all, I need something much less ornamental,
I seek something natural, organic, elemental.

Compared with religion, spirituality seems more palatable,
A recognition that in humans, a spark of mysticism exists.
The need to feel part of something larger,
In my life still persists.

Commentary on Belief

I am an atheist. I do not believe in God, a Creator or anything of that type. So, by definition, I fit that description. I do not decry the right of others to believe and, in fact, I respect anyone's right to believe whatever they wish, but I do expect the same in return. Personally, I have quite negative views of organised religion, but that doesn't mean I am prepared to ignore the spiritual.

I think when many of us recognise that definition of the atheist in ourselves, we think that also means a loss in being able to claim any interest in spirituality and or spiritual practice. To explore what is meant by spirituality in the context of being an atheist, I found an interesting website, *The Mortal Atheist*, which focuses on 'Secular Discussions About Mortality and Meaning'. In an article *Spirituality for Atheists* published on that site on 26 June 2023, it concludes:

"Three ways to think about spirituality for atheists. The first is the expanded sociobiology of belonging—a desire for connectedness that extends to the natural world and the cosmos (oneness). The second is our yearning for there to be more to life than death, more to life than our lifespan (transcending physical reality).”

“The last is the rational pursuit of an honest worldview, which includes cutting through the illusion of a separate 'self' (a quest for fundamental truths). Spirituality for atheists, then, can be about connection, continuity, and contemplation without chafing against reason or requiring belief in souls, destiny, 'energy', or other dubious concepts.”

“You can also see why we shouldn’t discard spirituality as supernatural absurdity, as unessential or unimportant. Belonging and mortality are existential concerns, and most atheists are already persuaded of the vitalness of truth and analytic inquiry.”

“Sceptics shouldn’t dismiss spirituality as nonsense, for it needn’t be irrational nor religious. Instead, spirituality may be the most natural thing about us, the thing that truly does connect us to the cosmos, to the world, and to each other.”

This encapsulates my current feelings very well and may mark the beginning of further reading to allow me to better understand my own beliefs here. There are two books by Jordan B Peterson, I feel I might find interesting in my education: *Maps of Meaning* and *We Who Wrestle with God*.

It is striking too that some mycologists suggest that the rise in the use of psychedelic drugs as a consequence of using certain fungi might be linked to the mind-expanding aspects of these drugs and the founding of religions, and in appreciation for our place in the universe. That is a whole other side of exploration—probably best left to scientists and in hospitals—where research can progress whilst research participants can be better protected if there are any adverse medical events.

19 Nov 2024

A Mother's Love, a Son's Awe

The mystery remains,
A conundrum still,
How a mother overcame so much:
With insight, good decisions and strength of will.

How a mother single-handedly raised,
Six children and presided over,
Without becoming crazed,
The great success of her elder son.

And that son, coming home with a good education,
Wishes he'd been able to ask her how she'd done it;
The decisions taken, the sacrifices made.
The impetus? Perhaps in him, she saw her own spark lit.

This poem was written for Ako in memory of his mother by his friend, and fellow academic, Richard Godfrey. Ako and I have had many interesting conversations that have made us realise just how much we have in common: from science to family relationships and shared values. Ako, these things are just a few that encapsulate our friendship, and in that I rejoice.

With very best wishes,
Richard Godfrey

Commentary on a Mother's Love, A Son's Awe

The son referred to here is my friend, Ako, who is from Cameroon. He had five siblings. As the older son, in his culture, it was Ako's role to support his mother in looking after the family in the absence of his father, who died when Ako was just 12 years old. Some who have given me feedback on this poem have questioned the word 'elder' in the last line of the second verse, assuming I have made an error.

By using 'elder' rather than 'eldest', I hope to provide the reader with more information about the family. Ako never questioned my choice of words, but then he already knew the number of boys and girls. As a talented multi-linguist, however—who has worked teaching in English for a long time and who had worked for many years prior to this as a translator for the Cameroon Government—I am sure he was very comfortable with my deliberate word choice.

Introduction to Grimaldi's Proud Boast: A Narrative Poem

The following poem is the last in this collection, and if you have got this far, I am hoping you'll come on this last journey, a fantasy that originated in my mind. It differs from all other poems in this collection. It is, in effect, a short story and being longer than any other poem here, it will take longer to read.

We find ourselves currently in this world, dominated, conditioned by social and other media to expect and prefer 'soundbites', to get to the point quickly. But sometimes, delayed gratification can be very much more rewarding and, even, fun. I recommend that you read *Grimaldi's Proud Boast* through, completely in one sitting.

If you do so, it will take ten full minutes. Quite long by the standards of other poems here, but not in comparison with narrative poems generally. Examples of narrative poems include Alfred Lord Tennyson's *Morte d'Arthur* or the anonymous *Beowulf, or* the ballad style as demonstrated by the excellent *The Ballad of Reading Gaol* by Oscar Wilde.

I am not confident I could ever write in such a sustained way, as I perceive most narrative poems to be, and many extend to the length and epic nature of the novel. For a ballad,

The Ballad of Reading Gaol is long, has an excellent and altogether satisfying rhyming scheme.

Frankly, it is a work of genius, and I will never achieve anything like that quality of expression, powerful imagery, incredible skill in the use of language and an amazing ability to stimulate imagination!

It is probably a mistake to name names as I have done above, as to do so might give the reader the impression I am arrogant enough to believe I am equal to such company. I am not! I know I am not, and further, I know I never will be! I am simply an admirer and an aspirant. Perhaps my humble effort might persuade you to explore these, unlike me, entirely illustrious others.

And yet I allow myself here the luxury of both an introduction prior and a commentary after! So, perhaps my arrogance is beginning to stretch its current boundaries! I'll let you be the judge, but first, I really hope you enjoy my attempt at an 'extended' poem that I like to imagine is a narrative poem.

Grimaldi's Proud Boast

Into the west and the setting sun,
Go Grimaldi's men, tired,
But their toil's just begun.

Leaving their loved ones, they marched.
A day and a night,
Over mountain and valley,
They'd soon spy the sea,
In the land of the red kite, they'd presently be.

On a cold battlefield, frost underfoot;
Encamped for the night,
Quiet but for owls that hoot.
No sleep to refresh even one tired bone,
The approaching dawn fight for that single prized throne.

In dawn's twilight calm, many awoke with a fright,
Dreams of happier times left in the night.
To rise as the cock crows,
Shaking with fear;
No comforting word in your ear.

With small comfort from food,
Rank upon rank lined up with their comrades;
And stared at enemies and brothers.
All sides of men thought of their families, their mothers.

The smell of woodsmoke fills the air,
In the dawn's early light.
With fear and cold, hands tremble and shake,
Ordered to give no quarter, no prisoners to take.

Up goes a shout,
A horseman rides the line;
Not long now, all hope they will be fine.
Unto the breach and beyond,
A battle in mud and blood, no time to yawn.
A victory lost, a victory won,
No pleasure found, even satisfaction they'd shun.

A compassionate life? A compassionate death?
For General Grimaldi, there was no winning.
A sword, a knife, a cutlass, a spear,
On that field, he lies dead and grinning;
Throat cut from ear to ear.

Ambition be damned and cast asunder,
A flash of lightning and a roll of thunder,
Mark that sad day,
Misled men, lying, many hearts, cut away.

A sea fog rolled in at the end of the day,
And all through the night, a wailing was heard;
Grimaldi's ghost left to wander alone,
A punishment for evil lust for a throne.

His men returned home,
But their minds they had lost;
Left back on that battlefield,
And caked in mud, blood and frost.

Cursed to live amongst the living,
Men without souls,
With no hearts for forgiving.
The womenfolk weep for the men they have lost,
And the minds left back there,
In the mud, blood and frost.

To build a future full of hope, love and zeal,
To gods who forsake them,
They make a grand appeal.

But soon to discover,
A means to make wounds heal;
Let go of the past,
For the future: bells peal.

"But how did we get here
To live in such stench and decay?"
Asked one young lad,
Missing the father he no longer had.

The old recalled stories from memories dim;
Of greed, lust and envy,
Of corruption-led zeal,
But truth grows dimmer with each turn of the wheel.

An old man with a faraway look in his eye,
Stares into the fire, searching for a place to begin,
To relate the tale of one young man's whim.

One long, last look back,
Thirty years whence it began.
Back to that time,
Grimaldi, a handsome young man.

His eyes, they shone with naked ambition,
But soon the land he'd lead toward attrition.
In awe and humility, common folk knelt,
And presented to him many a fine pelt.

But this man was sculpted in childhood days,
When showered with inappropriate praise,
For cruel selfish acts, his mind, in a haze.

A cosseted child who could do no wrong,
But for recognition and fame did he constantly long.
And as he grew older, so his confidence did too
Whilst with rose coloured vision, his parents would view,

A son, fine and strong, of whom they were proud;
But ignoring the behaviour they noticed,
But from others would shroud.

Yet soon, growing confidence became arrogance,
Convinced of his destiny,
At the less worthy down his nose, he would glance.

In first conflict, he goaded a man to a fight;
A man four times his age, not long for this life,
He murdered him quickly, in front of his wife.
In his mind, his status did grow,
But unknowingly, headed for purgatory, his soul he did throw.

And onward to darkness his destiny bound.
Slowly, he changed; those who knew him frowned.
But behaviour is subtle, and many would miss.
The things that would steer him from a life full of bliss.

As a youth, in summer, his blond shoulder-length hair,
And a slight build marked him out;
As few had, but dark hair and many were stout.

At 16, a royal princess he met,
And suggested to her that with him alone she slept.
For the first time, he encountered rejection outright;
And murdered her there, but with no conscience did fight.

No real proof did the king possess,
But couldn't have Grimaldi stay;
He knew of the rumours,
And must send him on his way.

So, leaving Grimaldi no time to react,
The king took action, bold and fast,
To rid the land of this man of avarice,
To let no further regret come to pass.

Of honest men you seldom hear,
Tales of evil men abound.
This story will be ever told,
As history repeats itself, I've found.

So, banished from that land with force,
Grimaldi beat a hasty retreat.
But still, he saw his future there; this land of milk and honey,
And he would suck long from the teat.

On his departure, he'd threaten and strut,
And promised to take the throne was his boast,
Plunging the land into chaos,
With the king's blood would he toast?

Then quickly into another land,
He slipped without notice,
And found a friendly people there,
Ignorant of his evil deeds, but that mantle now was his.

So, in that land, he courted support,
And as their trust grew,
They came to respect his actions,
And thought their interests were his too.

In that land was their loyalty cultivated,
But slowly, he'd stir hearts and fears;
And worked hard to trick the people,
Enjoying life there for many years.

A leader of the common folk,
Amongst them, he rose to fame;
Yet still that evil spark lay hid,
Dark ambition he could never tame.

His dreams he could see arising,
Growing before his eyes,
No trouble to use these proles;
No conscience in these ties.

With rousing talk of an embittered land;
Far beyond the river, beyond that broad horizon,
Falsely accused of imminent invasion;
An evil lie of his devising.

His aim was clear,
To himself alone;
To steal that land;
To have that throne.

To have revenge on a king,
Who dared take a stand,
When many years ago,
He'd banished Grimaldi from that land.

With powerful oratory,
He turned every mind.
And soon with hatred,
Each dawn with malice, they'd find.

They believed his fabrications.
Following him into battle,
And, blind to reality,
Slaughtered all innocents in a defenceless village, like cattle.

Drunk with victory,
Their belief in him grew.
Acknowledged as their general;
Of truth? Only he knew.

So, they followed him to war.
And marched for many days.
And believed they went in the name of right;
In reality, still blinded by a haze.

Into the west and the setting sun,
Went Grimaldi's men,
To fight, they thought, in honoured battle,
To return home? Not one knew when.

Many battles they fought,
Many innocents they slaughtered,
But doubts? They grew,
With every woman and child, they slew.

One man had a cousin in that land,
Another had an uncle;
They told the truth of old,
And Grimaldi was revealed,
Once the whole story was told.

So, almost ends my tale of woe.
Of a soul grown corrupt,
Of the guile and evil of avarice,
Of one who would always seek the overflowing cup.

Of the horrors of war,
In an unworthy cause,
With no time for thought,
With no sensible pause.

No war provides a winner,
Any victory can only be hollow;
Too much death and destruction,
Too much ill will to swallow.

But Grimaldi left a son,
Who, in the absence of a father, is cosseted.
With the intellect of the father bold,
The next chapter of this tale, just waiting to be told.

Riding the steppe,
Is a young thug in the making,
Who taunts children and women,
In whom great evil is waking.

But many a year sees a spark lie dormant,
Yet still enough evil;
He cultivates skills of torment.

Do you lie in your bed still and quiet,
And imagine your life is your own,
When evil lurks all the while,
Jealous eyes on your home?

We all know a Grimaldi,
His dynasty lives still,
Yet often covert, they stand not on the hill.

Beware great oratory,
Oh, how it all makes sense.
But can lead us all to a life more intense.

Where tolerance is rare;
Soon, innocents stand accused,
And paranoia is the one thing left we share.

Commentary on Grimaldi's Proud Boast

I have no real idea where this poem came from! It seemed to have a life of its own, driving me on, taking four days to complete all fifty-nine verses. I didn't eat much, and when I did, it was only to snack. I didn't want the distraction from writing.

Even sleeping was no more than three hours on each of three nights because the poem consumed me. I might even say it controlled me; it took me over with a desire to tell a story, and yet, for most of it, I didn't know what it was about, or even what the story was, probably until the last three or four verses.

I gave it the title of *Grimaldi's Proud Boast*. I didn't know who Grimaldi was, why I gave him that name or what his boast was, until I stumbled upon it around halfway through!

The events of the poem are, clearly, set in an earlier time when cutting and stabbing weapons were the weapons of war and battles were fought on foot and on horseback, on the 'steppe'. So, it seems to take place in some Eurasian kingdom in mediaeval or similar times. I didn't plan to write about such a period in history; it just felt appropriate, and so I went with it.

In writing it, I was simultaneously juggling two difficult challenges: to maintain rhyme and rhythm in the immediate 'vicinity' of each word, each line and each verse, whilst also trying to think of the story without knowing, for most of four days, what the final story was going to be. And, dealing with those two things, at the same time, really was hard.

If I am asked to describe it, I will say:

I see it as a short story, moral tale, in the form of a narrative poem, and I wrote it in 2006, a year before I had a heart attack. So, the best part of almost two decades had passed, and I have been unable to write any further 'short story narrative' poems. It was just so monumentally difficult. The poem is not perfect; some verses are three lines long, some are four, and others are five.

It would be nice if each verse were consistently four, six or even eight lines long. I have seen the narrative poems of other poets and was impressed by one that was the length of a whole book with nice, neat eight-line verses. Is the fact that my poem does not have an even number of lines a valid criticism? I really don't know. The rhyme is imperfect, but I think the rhythm is quite good, although it is not necessarily constant, which I don't think is a real problem.

In fact, that has allowed me to emphasise certain thoughts, ideas and events and perpetuate discomfort in parallel with a tale which is frankly, unsavoury. It is evocative, I hope. I think the story is quite good and so is the moral, which, I hope, leaves the reader thinking, reflecting for a while afterwards.

I don't think it was ever contrived; it 'controlled' me or, at least, that is how it felt. If I were to try to write others of this type, something tells me they could only be contrived. I would like to write another, but I don't think it is in me! But who knows? Perhaps doing some homework on narrative poetry will help, but you still need a story!

Two questions to the reader:

1.   What was Grimaldi's boast?
2.   What do you think is the moral of this tale?

Index By First Lines

(**Line,** *title of poem,* ***page number***)

I gently consider truth in what I see, hear and smell. *Heart and Soul.*

I have no friends. *Betrayed by Most.*

I need not profound sadness. *The Meaning of Life.*

I shared some poems. *Why Did You Write Them?*

I sit alone in my dad's house. *Echoes of a Life Left Behind.*

I thought then, ending our relationship. *The Past: A Different Land.*

I was greatly loved. *Alone.*

I work to recover. *Haragei.*

I've been putting it off for weeks. *Bourne End Barbers.*

If you read my poetry, you will know. *Too Deep, Too Dark.*

In happier times, again we'll meet. *Sparkling Memories.*

In natural, breath-taking, verdant green. *Spring Woodland.*

In slow creeping cold. *Hope Springs Eternal.*

Insecta chatter, insecta call. *Flight.*

Into the west and the setting sun. *Grimaldi's Proud Boast.*

Is the process of writing. *Healing or Destroying.*

It is really too much. *An Early Year.*

It seems late in the day. *Belief.*

It was on a Monday. *Three-Day Week.*

It's not an easy 'true dat' thing. *New Era.*

It's thanks to a relative stranger. *Warning: Sense of Humour Failure.*

Let no one tell you. *Colour in Winter.*

Low, slow-rising cold. *Stark Winter.*

Mark liked stories! *Mark Harries.*

My arms are sore. *Post a Weight-Training Session.*

My chocolate addiction is fulsome. *Chocolate Addiction.*

My eyes pricked. *The Sting of Tears.*

No achievement, big or small. *Doubt and Fear.*

Perhaps no one should. *Job Sell-by Date.*

Perhaps surprisingly, the aftermath was overwhelmingly positive. *What Persists after my MI?*

Poetry has function. *Poetry Spectrum.*

Retreat deep into your inner self. *Aka-i.*

Run, run for the hills. *Got to Get Out of This Place.*

She was my dad's choice. *Rosemary.*

Some enjoy the darkness. *Darkness Magnifies the Light.*

Suddenly, my parents had no confidence. *Key Actions of My Mum and Dad.*

The cliff remains in sight and sound. *Seascape.*

The constant pain. *Hips: reflection 2023.*

The eagle's feather, the butterfly's wing. *Transients 2.*

The mystery remains. *A Mother's Love, A Son's Awe.*

The noise it builds. *Upper-crust Riverside Town.*

The whale looked. *Sperm Whale.*

The wheelhouse was warm and toasty. *Cruel Sea.*

There *are* nice people in this world. *Carve a New Niche.*

They've stopped listening. *The Question of Elder Wisdom.*

Today I walk London's. *Annual Haematology Check-up.*

Two wasps upon a window bright. *Two Wasps.*

Where hope triumphs over experience. *Hope over Experience.*

With ageing, you learn. *Solitude.*

You assume that we are like you. *Tarred With the Same Brush.*

You think you create a storm in me. *Ode to Greater Resilience.*